IT TAKES ALL KINDS

by

Florence Crannell Means

Florie wasn't pretty like her sister Coral, she wasn't bright in school, but she could tinker with cars and cook and clean the house when her mother couldn't be bothered. Only her cerebral-palsied brother adored her, she felt, and this made her drab life meaningful. Her teacher helped her pass her driver's test, which meant she could help her father in the junk business. When she got her first pretty skirt and sweater, and a bouquet of roses, Florrie found that she was a special person. A very realistic story about all kinds of people, which should make *everyone* feel lucky.

⚜

Classification and Dewey Decimal: Fiction (Fic)

About the Author:

As a child FLORENCE CRANNELL MEANS spent more time in her father's study than in her playroom. She divided her time between reading books and day dreaming of being a missionery, a writer, an artist. At the age of thirteen she moved with her family to Denver where she spent an outdoor life riding horses, catching toads and lizards and racing through the prairie with her dog. Her education consisted of high school, art school, studying Greek and philosophy with her father and taking college extension courses. With her husband, daughter and grandchildren, Mrs. Means spends her summers in the Rockies. Her interest in the people of the world has led her to spend much time with the Indians of the Southwest. In addition she has adopted children from China, Japan, Latin America and Burma. Mrs. Means finds life absorbing, believes that writing is more fun than anything imagined and what she wants her books to say is that regardless of color or race, folks are folks.

IT
TAKES
ALL
KINDS

FLORENCE CRANNELL MEANS

1967 FIRST CADMUS EDITION
THIS SPECIAL EDITION IS PUBLISHED BY ARRANGEMENT WITH
THE PUBLISHERS OF THE REGULAR EDITION
HOUGHTON MIFFLIN COMPANY
BY
E. M. HALE AND COMPANY
EAU CLAIRE, WISCONSIN

This book is dedicated to

Eleanor Hull

and

Mary DeLapp,

whose questing spirits

and racing feet

find Cochrane families

in New York and

in Suburbia.

1

FLORETTE COCHRANE shifted her little brother on her lap so that his thin body should not poke into her at so many points.

"Elvie more comfterble this way?" she crooned. "Hm?"

The old pickup truck was not easy riding for an all-day trip. The passengers in the back had especially rough going, for they were crowded in among the household goods that had overflowed from the trailer. The single seat was a little better, but Pop, Mom and Coral filled it full.

Sixteen-year-old Florette hardly noticed the jolting. In spite of everything she was happy. It was all because of something unexpected and beautiful that had happened that morning.

George Gaynor had come to bid them goodbye. In the chill gray dawn of early March he had driven his rickety jeep across the miles, getting there just as the sun came up and the five Cochranes were preparing to start away. It meant something, for George to come then. Florette hugged the thought to her now, smiling as she smoothed Elvie's silky curls.

1

The Nebraska farm and the ramshackle old farm-house were the only home Florette had known, and deserting them was like deserting a person. But of course the farm wasn't theirs any longer. The Mortgage had eaten it up. All Florette's sixteen years the Mortgage and Automation had been heartless monsters, threatening the Cochranes. The big farms around them had grown bigger, with an increasing number of powerful machines. In their midst, with a rusty tractor and two or three other machines that only Pop's ingenuity kept wired together and running, and with Pop to drive them and Florette to help, the shabby little farm had been slowly squeezed to death.

Their old neighbors had long ago given up the struggle and sold out. No one had been left to bid the Cochranes goodbye, except — Florette's heartbeats danced — except Georgie.

George Gaynor had gone to the same consolidated school as Florette and Coral. His father's farm was beyond the school, and Mr. Gaynor was still holding on to it — "holding on like grim death," Pop Cochrane often grunted. The place was as down-at-heel as the Cochranes', and George was as shabby as Florette. There was nothing striking about George, except that he noticed Florette.

When she was a little girl, things were different. Then all the boys wanted her on their ball teams. Now those same boys looked past her as if she weren't there at all, and the girls were as bad. Funny how much you wanted to be noticed.

So she had looked at George a great deal this past year, and betweenwhiles she had thought about him. He was just her age, and in her sister's grade. The other boys hovered round Coral, but George had more to say to Florette when he walked a piece with them after school. He would look sidewise at Coral, pert and pretty, as if he didn't know what to say to her, and he'd grow red and tongue-tied if she spoke to him. Then he'd say to Florette, "Lookit that jackrabbit. Sure going to town." Or, "I say, what a big pheasant! Now if I had my gun you could have pheasant for supper, if it was pheasant season."

"And if you could shoot straight enough to hit the side of a barn," Coral scoffed.

George never said much, but who cared for that? It was her, Florette, he talked to. He wasn't anything to look at. Even Florette hadn't noticed much except that his ears stood out, and he had acne, and his changing voice squeaked more than any other boy's in school. She thought of these things tenderly, because he was her friend.

And he had come at sunrise to bid her goodbye.

For a few minutes he stood around. Then he rushed to carry some last things out of the house. Coral said, "Oh, Georgie, for heaven's sake look where you're going!" and he turned crimson and stumbled over his own feet, falling into the back of the truck and banging the cab window with the bed slat he was lugging. Florette was just behind him and seemed to be the only one who heard the ominous crack. Maybe no one would notice until they were well on their way.

George shook hands with Mom and Pop, and fished a lollipop out of his pocket for Elvie. Then he said, "Well, guess I better be on my way. Take it easy, Coral. Don't let them give you any wooden nickels, Florette."

He swallowed hard, not looking at either girl. Then he stuck out his hand to Coral, while Florette looked the other way. Finally he shook hands with Florette, muttered "Abyssinia," and loped away. Florette thought his eyes were wet, like hers, though that was almost too much to hope. But the ache of saying goodbye to him was better than the emptiness of having no one to say goodbye to.

She and Pop were the only ones who hated leaving the farm. Not that Pop said anything. It was the way he looked back. Mom had patted her favorite rosebush and mumbled that if it was summer she would have taken along a cutting. But it was only Florette who had to crowd back the tears. Ramshackle as the old place was, it had been a shelter, and she had often needed a shelter.

Maybe in the new place, where they would be starting over fresh — maybe folks would pay attention to Florette, as Georgie had done. He had been all upset,

4

she thought, as she watched that cab window. It was really cracked, and they had not jolted over many miles before a corner of it came loose and clattered into the truck bed, barely missing Florette.

Pop said, "Now what the Sam Hill," and drew up on the shoulder of the road and examined the window.

It ended by his having them all get out while he removed the rest of the glass, cutting his hands in the process, and swearing vigorously. It was going to be a lot colder for the three in the cab, but it would have its advantages for Florette, because now she could hear them and talk to them if she had anything to say.

Coral, sharing the cab seat with Pop and Mom because she had insisted on wearing her new coat, ran a pink-tipped hand through her blowing hair. Coral's hair grew steadily lighter in the sun that tanned her skin till it was the color of buckwheat honey. Elvie was the only other Cochrane who had that kind of glistening pale yellow hair. Fifteen-year-old Coral was pretty, and she had nice, smooth manners when she was away from home where she needed them. And she was quick enough in school, not a bit like Florette.

"Pop," Coral was saying, "is this all the faster you can go? It's getting cold. And I can't hardly wait to see our new place. I'm sure glad we're getting into town at last. No chance for anybody out in the sticks, not unless they've got money."

5

Pop shifted in his seat. "It ain't exactly right in town, Corrie. Just at the edge of Barnett, like. Nicer that way, if you ask me. I'd feel like I was in a cage, spang in the middle of town. Where we are, you get a nice view of the prairie and the mountains."

"Oh — view." Coral dismissed prairies and mountains. "What color did you say our house was?"

Pop cleared his throat and fiddled with the steering wheel. "Figured I'd best leave you girls pick the color. A real glossy white might look good."

"Is there a garden, Jim?" Mom had sat humped together as if she didn't care whether school kept or not. "Bushes and flowers?"

"Good place for your posies," Pop answered, "when I get it fenced in."

"Anyway, it's a new start," Coral said. "Get away from that school — hayseeds like Georgie or rich kids that think they're the only ones on earth, and look down their noses at you because you haven't anything but a truck to get around in. A person might amount to something in a new place."

Probably Coral was right. But would there be a boy like Georgie, to pay attention to Florette?

"Look, Elvie," she said huskily, "see the pretty baby in the looking glass off beside Pop." Five years old wasn't really a baby, but when he couldn't talk or walk or feed himself — He was pretty, though, just as pretty as Coral, except for the way his mouth hung open and his head wabbled on his thin neck. Tendrils like new corn silk clustered over the whiteness of his forehead, and his big brown eyes were shaded by thick lashes. His little red mouth would have been like a picture baby's if it had ever been closed.

"See the pretty baby," Florette repeated, taking his limp little hand and waving it toward the reflection in the mirror until he giggled. Everyone said he had no sense, but Florette was sure they were mistaken. Or why would he laugh in the right places when she talked to him and told him stories?

She studied the two reflected faces, pressed cheek to cheek. She hadn't much sense herself, she thought, except for machines and farmwork. Books — it seemed as if she couldn't make head or tail of them. Back there in the consolidated school she had taken two years to every single grade, so that now, at sixteen, she was only in seventh, while Coral, fifteen, was in ninth. Florette had long ago given up trying. What was the use? All those teachers thought she was retarded, and they ought to know.

And certainly she wasn't pretty, like Elvie and Coral. She was kind of heavy looking, and all the same color, brown hair, skin, eyes. Sometimes she thought it wasn't fair of God to give her so little chance, and Elvie none at all.

But Georgie had saved her to the last, when he said goodbye, as if she were something special. Maybe she

7

wasn't so bad-looking. Her nose was a good shape, and her teeth were straight and white. Maybe Georgie would write to her —

"Pop, you said we'd have a real car to go to Barnett in," Coral complained as the truck jolted over a stretch of rough pavement.

"Will you hush up, Corrie? The little bit them robbers gave me for the house and cows and the junk, it never added up to no fancy auto. Done pretty good to buy us a piece of ground and a house, if you ask me. But with the new business and all, it won't be no time before I can find us a car that I can tinker up so's we can ride in style."

"Seems like you might tell us what the new business is," Coral fretted.

"Just you hold your horses." Pop was working his neck around in his limp blue collar as if it hurt him. Florette studied its crisscross of wrinkles. When he wriggled that way he wasn't feeling too easy inside. "Rome wasn't built in a day," he said. "I mind that was in my copybook, years and years ago."

"Well, anyway," Coral repeated, "any place is better than the sticks. I get a chance to be somebody, once we're in town."

Yes, maybe Coral would get a chance, but what about Florette? Would the change be better for her? Or worse?

And what about Elvie? Would he be happy in town,

8

without little animals to watch, and maybe with strangers staring at him if Mom let him out of the house?

"S'pose you change places with me and drive a while, Florrie. Then I can stretch out and snooze. My back's cutting up fierce, and this cold wind don't help it none."

"But Elvie — ?"

"Elvie can just as good take his nap alongside his pop."

2

THE RIDE was like one of those dreams in which you are trying to go somewhere, and go on and on but never arrive. Florette's thoughts made the jolting and the chill bearable. If Georgie liked her well enough to come over and say goodbye, why shouldn't other folks like her, too?

Afternoon crept along, with each hour chillier than the last. The truck rumbled and jerked, and the home-made trailer clattered and jerked behind it. They crossed miles of prairie, much of it desert, inhabited only by the ghosts of last year's weeds. Elvie yawned and his head bobbed heavily against Florette, who was taking her turn in the back while Pop drove again. Fighting to keep awake, the child blinked up at his sister with sleep-heavy eyes. Florette hugged him. He was the only person who had it harder than she. Oh, Pop and Mom didn't have it easy, but they were old, past forty and past thirty.

"Look, baby," Florette coaxed. "Let Sister make you comfy and then you watch for bunnies and gophers."

10

"That reminds me," Pop called back to her: "there's a little colony of prairie dogs not so far from our new place. Gettin' right scarce, those little fellers."

Elvie widened his eyes at the gray-brown countryside as he lay against Florette's breast.

"Pop, I'm starved as well as frozen," Coral complained.

"Kind of peckish myself, now you mention it," he grunted, and drew up before the next filling station. After he had carefully counted some coins that he pulled from his pocket, he clambered down stiffly, stamping his feet to warm them. He soon returned with five chocolate bars.

Mom roused enough to nibble at hers, food being one of her few interests. Florette broke off small pieces and popped them into Elvie's mouth, opening wide like a baby robin's. She alternated bites for Elvie with bites for herself. She hadn't known she was so hungry.

Dusk was thickening when they came over a rise in the rolling plains, and Pop waved a dramatic hand ahead. "There is the lights of Barnett," he declaimed. "There is the Cochranes' new home."

Florette liked the prospect. At their right stretched the Rocky Mountains, a blue wall capped with white. Nearer at hand lay alternating desert and farmland with little houses nestling under bare dark trees. Buttes, like baby hills, poked up from the plains, and up ahead those city lights, pale in the twilight, but steadying and

11

brightening as night fell. They began to look like the church Christmas tree at home.

The truck passed the farms and came to a region of scattered small houses, sitting as if dropped helter-skelter on the bare plains. It came to a great cavity, with a light smoke rising from it, and a mingling of acrid odors.

Just beyond this, Pop slowed the truck and turned it, noisily protesting, to the right.

"Something broke?" Coral demanded. "Out of gas?"

Pop laughed, again wriggling his neck. "No, not a thing busted this time. And we had enough gas to take us all the way."

"But why are you stopping at a dump? It is a dump?"

"Yeah, it's a dump. And it's where your pop's new business is at. And this here's our new home."

Nobody said a word. They all sat and stared at the house. Half the size of their rambling old farmhouse, it stood huddled in the middle of nothing.

Snorting, Pop clambered down and began to slide things out of the trailer. "Ain't you got nothing better to do than sit there like bumps on a log? You, Florrie, can't you shake a leg and help tote?"

Florette said, "Mom, if you'll take Elvie. He's gone to sleep."

Mom heaved herself out of the truck and took the limp body. Only Coral remained, staring through the

12

deepening twilight at the house, shivering convulsively and pounding the seat with her fists.

"Pop Cochrane," she shrieked, "you're kidding. That can't be our nice new house. It's nothing but a — a chicken coop. And smack on the edge of that smelly dump. I won't stay here. I'll run off."

"That's no way — to talk to — your father, Coral Cochrane." Pop was puffing under the weight of two mattresses. "And as for — the house — it's a — right solid little house, and — when I've — nailed up some loose — boards, and — painted it — "

Florette said, "Mercy to us, Pop, couldn't you find nothing better than this?"

But Pop likely felt as if he was alone, with all his folks against him. Florette said, "Sure, we can all pitch in and paint, and you wouldn't hardly know it for the same place, Corrie. And, like you said, Pop, it's real pretty with the mountains off there."

Pop slammed his mattresses down on the porch, trying to avoid the jagged hole in the floor. Breathing stormily, he fished a key from his pocket, unlocked the door, squeaked it open, and tugged in his mattresses, Florette following with another.

"In the next room," Pop grunted. "Put 'em on the floor. For the present."

Mom deposited Elvie on one of the mattresses, and the three of the Cochranes trudged in and out, lugging bedding and boxes.

13

"Best get all the good stuff inside," Pop said. "No way to lock the trailer."

"Fat chance anybody'd want such junk," Coral whimpered from the truck seat.

"You march yourself in and help, young lady," Pop growled, but paid no attention when she paid none.

"Whyn't you turn on the lights, Jim?" Mom asked. "Can't see where to stick things."

Pop stood still, clasping a box of food. "No bulbs," he snarled. "Ain't candles good enough for you one night? I used 'em, night I camped out here after I bought the place. Had the electricity turned on next day, but didn't get no bulbs. You'll find some candles in the kitchen cupboard. Matches, too."

When Florette had fetched the candles and lighted them, she giggled. "Makes us all look like Halloween ghosts."

Pop thumped her shoulder. "Sure like a good sport," he praised. "Pity the rest of you have to be so meeching."

"I wouldn't feel so all gone if I had a hot cup of tea," Mom muttered, shivering violently.

"I'll light the gas and get the kettle boiling," said Florette, cheered by Pop's unusual praise. "It is gas, I reckon?"

"Coal and wood. We'll lay in some tomorrow. Sure don't feel like rassling any tonight. Cold food never kilt nobody. We got crackers left, and there's a can of cold meat, ain't there? You open it up and I'll go out and pump us some fresh water. We got a well real close to the door. Good water, too."

Elvie woke, and set up a hiccuping wail.

"Hush that noise," snapped Coral, who had at last come in and stood glaring around her. "Top of everything else, you got to begin yowling."

"He's cold," Florette angrily defended him, handing can and opener to Mom and picking him up from the mattress. "And wet, isn't it, baby?"

She soon had him dry, and had chafed his cold little hands and feet and snuggled him in a sweater.

The evening stillness was broken by the squawk-squawk of the pump and presently Pop came slopping in with two pails of water. Florette fumbled in the dimness for a cup, filled it full and held it to Elvie's gulping, spattering mouth. Then she wetted a rag and wiped the chocolate from his face.

"Well," said Pop, "grub ready? Already got two chairs without unloading the rest of the trailer. Off of the dump. You kids can hunker down on the floor to eat."

Coral stood holding a paper close to the flame of one of the candles, which brightened her hair into a halo above her frowning face.

"What's that you're reading, Corrie?" asked Pop, mouth full of meat and spraying cracker crumbs.

Scornfully Coral waved the paper — notebook paper,

15

from the holes along its edge. "Listen to this and get a good laugh. 'I only hope you won't get too grand, living in a new house in the city. I hope sometimes you'll remember the old friends who thought so much of you back on the farm. Oh, Coral, won't you write to me? I always did think you were the cutest, prettiest girl in the whole world.'"

Florette held a cracker sandwich a few inches from Elvie's reaching mouth and stared at her sister. For the first time she noticed the deep chill of the house. It made her feel like leaves she had seen, coated with ice.

"Too grand! New house! A dump on the dump!" Coral burst into furious tears.

"You been keeping a sweetheart hid from your folks?" Pop snarled, eyes glinting.

"Sweetheart!" Coral screamed. "I wouldn't touch that George Gaynor with a ten-foot pole."

Numbly Florette thrust cracker and meat toward Elvie's mouth. When he pushed it toward her own lips, she obediently took a bite, though it would hardly go down her throat.

She should have known.

3

THAT NIGHT was something out of another bad dream. As soon as they had eaten, the Cochranes brought in the pillows and all the comforts and quilts from the trailer, which Pop drew up close to the house for the safety of its remaining contents.

By this time the cold was so intense that he brought in a few packing boxes and built reluctant fires in cookstove and small heater, and they pulled the mattresses into the area that was a little thawed by the feeble glow. Though Mom still murmured about making a cup of tea, they were all tired enough to drop down on their pallets with their clothes on, and huddle under mountains of covers.

Before long Florette could hear her father's unmistakable snore, like a steam boiler working up to the explosion point, held there a moment, and then starting over again. Mom's was like a stopped-up teakettle. Coral whimpered and muttered in her sleep, and Elvie burrowed closer to his sister and was lost in a deep slumber.

Florette stayed awake — not actually thinking, only feeling. Well, they must be right when they said she hadn't any sense. How could she ever have thought that any boy would want to look at her? Especially when Coral was around. She wished she could cry, but no tears came. She heard a scratching in the woodwork. Mice. An odor breathed through the house. Did skunks know how almost everyone despised them? She hoped they didn't, poor things.

She drew up her icy feet and tried to tuck the quilts tighter around her and Elvie. At least he was a warm bundle against the middle of her. Soon her curled-up legs were so cramped and aching that she had to straighten them, and leave them till they felt as if an icy stream were running over them.

She had little moments of dreams, never sure that they were dreams, nor whether she were awake or asleep. After an eternity of freezing and rolling into a ball, and aching and unrolling, the thin light of dawn stole in through the ragged shades Coral had jerked down last night.

The battered little clock stood on the windowsill where she had put it. It said two-thirty. Nobody had wound it. The eastern horizon was red with the coming sunrise, so now, in early March, it must be after six. Florette detached herself from Elvie, tucked the covers closer around him, and stole to the front door, treading softly, not to disturb the others. The floor creaked, in spite of her caution, and for a moment she poised, breathless. No one stirred, so she eased open

18

the creaky door, slipped through, eased it shut behind her.

She took a deep swallow of frosty morning. The house faced east, with a wide view of rolling land, broken by few trees. The sun was rising in fiery splendor that kindled the day. One leafless tree was drawn in black ink upon the red and gold.

An occasional car sped by toward Barnett, but for the most part Florette had the world to herself. She liked such times. The sky was for her, and the great prairie. The air was wonderful except for the taint of smoke from the dump. The skunk smell was good, if you only thought of it that way. A little like sage or catnip.

She stood straighter and filled herself as with an icy drink. Seemed as if God must really like folks, or else why would He have taken the trouble to make things so neat and right — and so beautiful? She could think of Georgie now without its hurting so bad. It was not so much that it was Georgie, but that it was someone who had singled her out and liked her.

And now there was nobody.

Well, she reckoned she couldn't be so hungry if she had a broken heart. Georgie's appealing brown eyes gave place to pancakes hot from the griddle — hot! — and swimming in oleo and molasses. Convulsively she swallowed.

The house remained so still that she knew they were all asleep. Why shouldn't she build a little fire out here behind the house, and get water boiling for coffee? Why not have a cookout breakfast?

Stepping softly from the rickety porch, she began to hunt for wood. Maybe Pop wouldn't mind if she broke up another packing box. She found a small one that he had emptied last night and carried it out behind the house as far as she thought their lot might go, not to disturb the sleepers. At the same time she kept at a distance from the outhouse, which was anything but savory. She whanged the box down on a rock so that it broke apart and she could lay the ends and sides one by one across her ragged denim knees and break them with a satisfying crash.

Apprehensively she looked at the back door. Yes, it squeaked open and Pop stood there, yawning, flinging wide his arms, blinking at her. With a glance over his shoulder he came down the steps and strode toward her across the brittle prairie grass, swallowing his yawns and shrugging his sweater higher around his neck.

"Brrrrr. Cold. What you up to, kid? Aiming to wake the folks? When they're asleep, seems like that's the only time they ain't on my neck, your mom and Corrie."

Florette shook back the heavy hair from her eyes. "Can't we build us a little fire out here, Pop? I fetched along some cold boiled spuds in a pail. And there's that sausage — "

Pop gulped. "Sure sounds good to me, Florrie.

20

Might look kind of crazy, cooking in the back yard, but they say the swells do it, these days. You fix up the spuds and I'll build the fire. Reckon we won't be needing these packing boxes no more — " He ambled over to the trailer and pulled out a heavy one.

"Wouldn't that make a table or something?" Florette asked, against the advice of her stomach, which was expectantly churning at the thought of food.

Pop said, "We'll get the table and chairs, kid. All in good time," and made the big case screech its farewell to the world.

"My land," complained Coral as Florette sliced the potatoes and got out cakes of sausage from the crock, where it had been stored in its own fat since they made it last winter. "My land, can't you let a person get a wink of sleep?"

"A person better get up and wash herself for breakfast," Florette retorted. "You put on too much lipstick yesterday. It's all over your face."

Pop's fire was going now, with a stream of sparks and much crackling. Florette sniffed the tang of burning wood as she ran out to make use of it, carrying a frying pan and the sausage and potatoes. Pop fetched the other frying pan and a fistful of sliced bread.

"Leave me have some of that grease," he said. "Fried bread ain't nothing to be sneezed at."

The sausage was soon snapping and sending out a mouth-watering aroma. It sent out also a blistering

21

spatter for Florette's hands as she lifted it out on a pie plate and poured some of the fat into Pop's skillet. "Darn, darn, darn," she scolded at the stinging little burns.

"Got to give it your mom for her sausage," Pop grudged, licking his lips. "She's a master hand with the seasoning. I've always heard that good eaters is good cooks. We ain't had much chance to prove it lately."

By the time the potatoes were browning and a stack of the fried bread rose high on another pie plate, Mom and Coral had appeared, clutching their sweaters around them while they grumbled about some folks' crazy notions, and hunched themselves closer to the grateful warmth.

"You leave some for when Elvie wakes up," Florette urged as she poured out the crisp rounds of potato.

"No coffee?"

Mom's complaining voice rasped across Florette like sandpaper on a match. "Mercy to us," she exploded. "Mom, can't you even fix your own coffee? Or can't Coral?" But having flared out at them, she ran in, slamming the door each time she went through, and brought out a battered pot with water and coffee. That fragrance was soon added to the others.

"I've read that rich folks has their coffee after they've et," Pop said amiably. "Us Cochranes must be rich folks. Don't know but we are, at that: got our own house and lot. And no mortgage."

Coral hooted with bitter laughter. "House and lot, my eye. Well, I only hope if I get acquainted with some nice kids at school, they won't ever see this dump. Hope they don't find out my father is a junkman."

"Your father is no junkman." He glared at her over the rim of his tin cup. "Your father is a hauler, and I'd like to know why hauling isn't a respectable trade."

"And this house," Coral wailed, undiverted. "It's even worse than the one back home. And ugly as sin. And dirty. And not room to turn around in it."

"Corrie — " Pop's tone was lofty — "you have to look ahead. You know what your pop sees? He sees a real white house, shining proud and pretty in a green yard with posies. And inside a year I aim to build on, so we can all have more room. There ain't no end to what we can build on," he added largely, smiling at the huddled gray house as if it were already a mansion.

"Can we start painting right off?" Florette asked.

"Hold your horses, girl. Rome wasn't built in a day. Looks like when I've laid in a supply of wood and coal and grub, we got to sing small till the hauling begins to pay off."

"And furniture?" Coral demanded. "Bedsteads and chairs and a table? Or do you want us to live on the floor—and get splinters?"

Pop smiled triumphantly. "That's one of the good points about being a hauler. Them rich folks throws out the swellest stuff. I got them two chairs offen the

23

dump, and they don't need hardly anything but a few nails and some paint. And once I'm hauling it'll be even better. I'll get my pick of the discards before they even get to the dump."

Florette wondered whether Pop really would hammer in the nails and put on the paint. He would have changed a lot if he did much fixing around the house. But of course, Florette reminded herself, you couldn't have blamed him much. He wasn't very hefty, and he'd always had more than he could do, with nobody but Florette to help him.

"First off," Pop was rubbing his hands together as if everything were in full swing, "you girls could scrub the floors. Woodwork is smeary, too."

"And have you looked at the wallpaper?" Coral inquired. "Want us to scrub the wallpaper?"

"Oh, that." Pop dismissed the wallpaper as he drained another cup of coffee. "We'll yank it all off. It's loose anyway, and sort of hanging."

"Them greasy floors won't come clean without plenty hot water," Mom interposed. "And every drop to be pumped and then heated on the stove."

Pop stood up and stretched again. "Soon as it's time for the stores to open I'll go get us some coal and wood."

"You don't expect me to scrub that filthy floor?" Coral inquired, holding out her smooth hands and pink nails. "You know how bad I have eczema or something."

24

"Will it give you eczema to get Elvie and look after him just once in a dog's age?" Florette asked in her turn. "There he is, at the door."

"Elvie just hates me," Coral said, with a bitter glance at the child, who had managed to creep and roll to the door and was staring at them.

"He knows who loves him," Florette answered, and ran to scoop him up and cuddle him till he giggled and sputtered. "Know something?" she whispered in his ear. "You're the only one in the world who likes me best."

4

The scrubbing was a messy, dirty job, yet it was not without its advantages, since Florette kept a fire going in the kitchen stove to heat the many buckets of water. It was the first time since their arrival that they had been comfortably warm.

Mom worked languidly, puffing because it was so hard to get her soft bulk down on the floor and up again. Coral used a mop in one of the rooms, inspecting her hands with attention each time she wrung it out.

"Whyn't you wash paint instead of floors?" Florette suggested.

"Paint? Where's any paint?"

"Well, what there is will look better clean."

Florette liked to work — when she had to work — with all her might; it felt better that way. The only times she paused today were to look after Elvie, and occasionally to watch what was going on at the dump. She could see a good deal while she emptied one bucket of dark suds after another, well back of the house.

Each loaded truck stopped at a tiny house at the entrance, Pop said to pay the dumping fee. Then they drove around to a high ridge on the far side and emptied their loads down a steep declivity: big, vanlike vehicles, and moderate-sized ones, and a few as small as Pop's pickup.

Even with these pauses, Florette scrubbed two of the four rooms herself, and helped set up Pop and Mom's iron bedstead, with its impressive brass balls, in a corner room. With quilts and pillows it looked comparatively inviting. A double mattress and a single one had been laid on the damp floor in another room. Coral would not sleep with anyone, and especially, she said, not with Elvie.

From a little store a mile away Pop brought wieners and potato chips and Coke, and they ate hungrily. But they'd got to go awful easy with the money, Pop warned them, because till the telephone was connected and they had an ad in the paper, they couldn't get much in the way of hauling. Come Monday he might canvass for jobs, but that would be slim pickings.

Next day was Sunday. Florette had sighted a small, spired building within walking distance. She and Coral had gone to church back home. Usually. So she asked Pop what kind of church it was.

Pop shrugged. "How would I know? Don't reckon it makes much difference what brand it carries. All supposed to go to the same corral. Only mighty few of the critters keep to the trail very good."

27

"Maybe that way we'd get acquainted quicker," Florette said. "You and me, Corrie, in case Mom and Pop don't want to go."

"Not me." Coral was inspecting her scratched hands. "It will take me all day to do my hair and my nails and get a dress washed and ironed for school."

She did use most of Sunday for those tasks, plus a thorough perusal of some old comic books.

Florette spent most of her time with Elvie. He was the one who needed her attention. For a child who could not walk and who could not creep at all well, he was able to get away remarkably fast; and here the prairie stretched out invitingly. The dump, with its smoke and its flickering flames, was even more tempting to a child fascinated by fire. Florette worked a long time, making a rope leash that would hold him securely and not draw up and pinch him. Finally she had him hitched to a staple that she drove into the back steps, so that he could crawl and roll in a wide arc and yet be kept from danger.

She also washed her hair, but she left it straight. Any way she tried curling it looked awkward.

Pop spent part of the day fiddling with his truck. He kept the engine clean as an engine could be, Florette thought. That was one thing you sure could say for Pop. He worked with the pump, too. It wasn't very dependable, but he would watch the dump and his own loads, and it was dollars to doughnuts he'd rake up some good substitutes for the worn-out parts. Florette hung over him while he worked, Elvie unleashed and astride her hip. She wished that books were as easy to understand as machinery.

"Florrie, seems a great waste for you to be a girl," Pop said. "You'd make a better boy, seems like. Way you took after me with your knack with machines, and using one hand just as good as the other, too. And I could sure use a boy."

"I'd be tickled to be a boy." Flushing, Florette thought that one good thing about being a boy was that you wouldn't have to hang back and wait for folks to make over you. Though maybe the Georgies ached inside, too.

"Florrie," Mom called from the doorway, "this TV's went haywire. Reckon you can tinker it up again?"

"That old loose connection," Florette said when she had peered into the decrepit workings of the instrument.

Pop's toolbox — the most orderly place in the whole Cochrane establishment — yielded the necessary tape, and when Florette had wound it deftly over the loose joining, the pictures began to flicker into view again. Mom established herself before it with Elvie, in the one rocking chair they had brought from the farm.

"Poor little tad," she said, smoothing his floss of bright hair. "He likes to see things moving and hear the racket. Listen at him giggle. Almost like he had

29

sense. Watch out, baby. You'll roll right off Mom's lap."

"Mom, it ain't just seeing things move and hearing the racket," Florette scolded. "He likes those funny cartoon figures, and they're what he laughs at. You do have sense, don't you, Florrie's little angel?"

"Just like a puppy or kitten," Mom said, kissing his white forehead. "Just God Almighty's little lamb."

Florette stamped an impatient foot. "I don't believe it. Some day Sister's going to take you to a big high doctor who knows everything, Elvie baby, and — "

"And get him took away from home and stuck in some nasty asylum? No, sir," Mom flared at Florette, pushing her away with a stockinged foot and bending over Elvie as if to hide him from a threatening world. "Elvie don't want to be took away from his mom and put in no asylum," she crooned, the easy tears oozing down her cheeks.

"Oh, you all make me sick," Florette muttered. Frowning, she settled herself on the floor and watched a fast-moving program noisy with gunshots and dizzy with cowboys and Indians, horses, and girls fresh from the beauty parlor. It swept her away from the rusty realities around her.

The small heater in the box of a living room joined forces with the cookstove to warm the house in the March cold, but before the young sheriff had arrived (in the nick of time) the air had grown close and odorous.

Florette jumped up, thrust her arms into the sleeves of her sweater and sought the outdoors. There it was much better. She walked along the nearer edge of the dump, looking at it curiously. It was a queer place, a great chasm in the level prairie, with that miniature mountain along one side, the place from which yesterday the haulers were dumping their loads.

She was glad it was not west of them, that high rim, where it would have spoiled part of their view of the Rockies. It didn't take much of a rubbish heap to shut out the tall mountains.

But if you could look at that chasm without smelling it, you could see something sort of pretty about it, with funny, changing colors. Only of course you didn't want to notice the piles of rags there at the foot of the miniature mountain.

Florette left the dump and struck out to the east, because Pop had said the new school was about a mile east of them. A chill wind was blowing, and she stuck her hands into her pockets and was glad she was wearing jeans. It was good to be alone. She let her heavy hair blow, and sniffed at the rich scent of sage. Trees and bushes crowded the edge of a ditch alongside the road, and as the lowering sun touched them they glowed with a warmer color than in winter. They would soon burst into the green flame of new leaves.

Out here in the open she couldn't keep on feeling prickly and dull and discouraged. The wind whirled round her till she felt like running and whooping. She did run, racing along, happier than she had been since night before last, when Coral had read George's letter aloud.

And maybe tomorrow, and school, would be fresh and new, like spring leaves.

Her flying strides petered out to a walk. She was approaching a farmhouse, and dogs were running to bark at her. It was the kind of house she and Coral had imagined theirs would be — How silly could you get? It sat, firm and comfortable, in a yard whose grass was already more green than brown, with trees arching over it and bushes embracing it. Its windows gleamed golden in the low rays of the sun, and its porch railing didn't lack a single shining spindle.

Still gazing at it, and paying no heed to the dogs now sniffing at her heels, she wheeled around and started up the long road toward home. She hadn't caught sight of the schoolhouse, the new school where tomorrow she might enter a brighter new world.

Or a darker old world. The wind had suddenly dropped, and so had Florette's spirits.

5

NEXT MORNING Pop took them partway to the new school. He could have taken them all the way, but Coral said, "Heavens, Pop! You think I want to be driven up in this old rattletrap?"

Pop's lips thinned. "In this old rattletrap and by this old pop."

"Well, you could anyway have shaved."

Florette gave him a clumsy pat as she got out. Pop did rile her, but maybe he was as easy hurt as anybody. He sniffed, and put the truck in motion the moment they were on the ground.

Coral was already scurrying ahead toward the big, many-windowed schoolhouse. With their flatness and their wings and their quantities of glass, schoolhouses looked alike nowadays, Florette thought. This one was a cousin of the one they had left.

Heart thudding with hope and fear, she lengthened her stride to overtake Coral's slim, scurrying feet. With a frowning glance over her shoulder, Coral quickened her running steps, and Florette fell back.

Now they were coming into a crowd of boys and girls. The smallest looked like babies, but must have been about twelve, since this was Kennedy Junior High. Florette felt more conspicuous than at the Nebraska school, for it held all grades and, at least on the school grounds, she could be lost among others of her age and size. One thing she was glad of: these kids were not all the stylish kind. Most of the boys wore jeans, and many of them jackets to match. The girls looked little better than Coral.

Coral went straight to the place where the office should be, and there it was. Florette quickened her trudging pace and caught up. Here there was no use Coral's pretending they were not together, with the same last name and all.

The young woman at the desk told them to go to the Girls' Counselor, Miss Farnsworth. "Right through that door," she pointed.

In the counselor's office Coral sat down with her usual flirt of skirts, and Florette perched on the edge of a chair the counselor indicated. "Your names and ages?" she asked, her eyes moving interestedly from one to the other.

"I'm Coral Cochrane" — Coral's voice was as dainty as her hair — "615 Jasmine." When Florette gave a muffled squeak of protest, Coral raised her voice a notch and repeated, "615 Jasmine. I am fifteen. And we came from Squaw Bluff, Nebraska."

"And this is your sister, I take it."

"My cousin," Coral corrected quickly. "Here is my report card. Give her yours, Florrie."

34

"You are in ninth grade, I see, Coral." Miss Farnsworth was studying the two cards. "And you, Florette? Is this correct? In seventh?"

Before Florette could answer, Coral put in, "My cousin has been sick a great deal. She was in the hospital five years."

How quick and smooth that Coral could make up her whoppers.

Miss Farnsworth smiled at Florette. "Sickness can upset everything, can't it? But you'll catch up, now you can be in school again. You look well now."

"Yes'm," Florette answered.

"Now you have a number of choices as to what studies you take," the counselor told them, sliding two typed sheets across to their side of the desk. "See: these courses you must take" — she pointed out a column on each page — "and these you can choose from. In your grade, Florette, you have English, arithmetic, physical education and geography or social studies. I notice the students call that Socks. And you can choose two more from those listed below. And in the ninth — " She went on with Coral's requirements and electives and turned back to Florette. "Selected yours, Florette?"

Sweat prickled out on Florette's forehead. "Art," she decided. "And is there gym?"

"Physical Ed is a requirement. Maybe Home Ec?"

Florette sighed her relief. "Yes'm."

"I see you have marked yours, Coral. Now you can

sign on the blanks indicated. Right there," she said, as Florette hunted over the page.

"The schoolbooks — there is a fee for them in Colorado, but if you didn't bring the money today, you can tomorrow. And for your gym suits."

"We'll bring it tomorrow," Coral said airily, while Florette wondered whether there was any to bring.

Next the counselor handed them each a sheaf of papers. "Take these home with you and read them carefully. Mr. and Mrs. Cochrane, too. They give information as to what Kennedy students are supposed to do or not to do. This one is to be signed by your parents or guardians, and this by yourselves. Now for your locker."

They followed her, and Florette watched attentively as she showed them the combination of the lock. She was much quicker than Coral about working it. "You use both hands," Miss Farnsworth said interestedly.

From the locker they went to their first classes, which by this time were being dismissed, and then to their second-hour classes.

"You'll finish the day in Miss Sansome's homeroom," Miss Farnsworth told Florette before she left her in her second class, with a notation of the next room numbers. "Miss Sansome is assistant counselor, and they don't come any finer."

Except for one thing, Florette would not have found the first day so bad, since the teachers let her alone to sit and look and listen. But whenever she encountered a new lot of little kids in a class, there were always some who stared at her and whispered behind their hands, and a few who snickered. You'd think I'd be used to it by now, she thought, but it just makes me wish I could die.

At the noon hour crowds of students poured down the stairs to the cafeteria. Florette got her sack from the locker and went with the rest, since the counselor had told them that home lunches also must be eaten in the dining room.

She did not catch sight of her sister until Coral emerged from the entry after school. Then she loitered along behind her, watching her wave gaily to the boys and girls they passed. Only when they had left all their schoolmates behind did Coral's pace slacken.

"Hi there, cousin!" she cried, laughing too hard.

"Afraid of the dogs, aren't you?" Florette responded stiffly. They were approaching another farmhouse where dogs yapped and roared.

"Dogs?" Coral arched her brows as if she hadn't noticed them. "Isn't it kind of fun to be cousins, Florrie?"

"Where's the fun about it? It's just hateful meanness, Coral Cochrane. And what's this about our living on Jasmine?"

"Well, we're near Jasmine. Didn't you notice the street sign? And there isn't any number on that — that

37

henhouse of ours." Coral's jaunty step had wilted, but her voice hardened. "You think I want them snooping around and finding out that we live on the dump?" She was pounding the air with balled fists. "They like me for a while. Every time new kids came to school the girls liked me for a while. But — " Her voice thickened with sobs — "what else can it be but that they find out what our house is like — and our family — ?"

"Pop and Mom and me and Elvie." Florette spoke unevenly, a hard, dull ache squeezing her heart. "I reckon Pop and Mom turn out to be your uncle and aunt. Or maybe they adopted you and we aren't any relation to you at all." Florette bit the insides of her cheeks to steady the quivering.

"Well," Coral grated, "since you mention it, I always did wonder. You and I couldn't hardly be less alike."

Florette did not try to answer. Certainly the sisters did not resemble each other. Florette had adored her sister's pretty daintiness, and had loved her devotedly until her love began to be tarnished by Coral's growing acidity toward her. Till she was about nine, Coral had accepted the older girl's homage like a small queen. Florette could still remember when a cool appraisal had crept into Coral's eyes. Luckily for Florette, Elvie was born at about that time, and helped tide her over the difficult change.

Mom hadn't been well after Elvie came, and ten-year-old Florette took most of the care of him. He needed a great deal of care.

"Boys are always slower than girls," Mom had kept insisting when Pop began to ask whether Florrie and Corrie weren't walking soon after they were a year old.

But when Elvie passed his second birthday and still could not hold up his wobbly head or say a word, even Mom had to admit that something was wrong. It seemed ironic that she had named him Elvis, after a popular young singer of the day, all strength and grace.

These thoughts traveled with Florette as the girls walked home. Sometimes she looked sidewise at her sister, who was worth looking at even when she was mad. Florette couldn't quite stop loving her, since she had started that way. And maybe when Coral grew up she would be nice again.

It was not until they approached their house that Elvie rolled into their sight at the end of his tether, uttering the cries that to Florette expressed delighted eagerness. This time it was not eagerness for his sister, but for something crawling on the ground, something on which he threw himself with a gurgle of triumph.

"Oh, it's a prairie dog," Florette said.

"Heavens!" cried Coral. "Elvie, turn loose of it! I've been reading — They can be sure death — "

Florette gaped at her, even as she poised to run, "How d'you mean? Bites?"

"No — an awful disease — "

Florette needed no more. Loping across the intervening space, she jerked Elvie backward by one leg, grabbed the little creature from beneath him, and flung it as far

39

as she could throw, while Elvie's giggles turned into howls.

"But how do you mean?" she asked her sister, who had stopped some distance away. "I never knew prairie dogs — "

"Oh, it's a horrible disease," Coral said, twisting her hands together. "You wouldn't understand. But one of these ground animals gets it, and then it bites another one — and the fleas come in somehow. Anyway they say to call the Board of Health if you see one that acts sick — "

Florette's gaze went from her sister to the small, gray-brown creature that lay still except for a slight twitching. "Yeah, it must be sick. That's how Elvie could catch it." She scrambled to her feet with the indignant Elvie.

"Don't you come near me," Coral warned. "Not till you've washed real good."

"Well, then, get me a basin of hot water. If there's any in the kettle. And soap. And a towel. And then you can fetch clean duds for Elvie. If he's got any. It's so warm in the sun I can wash him right here." She was stripping him as she spoke.

For once Coral ran, speedily bringing steamy basin, soap and towel, setting them down at a safe distance and hastily withdrawing. "I could get it myself," she chattered. "And die. Thousands of people — maybe millions — died in London — "

Florette hitched over to the basin with Elvie and scrubbed him vigorously, in spite of his angry yells and ineffectual kicks. "Thousands of folks? I don't believe it. It would have been on the radio."

Coral's shriek of scornful amusement was interrupted by Mom, who appeared in the doorway to demand an explanation of the activity.

"Oh, fiddlesticks," she protested, biting back her yawns. "Rubbish, if you ask me. They're always trying to keep folks hetcheled up. And anyways I been watching Elvie every minute."

Pop, when he came home, sided with the girls. "I seen something about that. In the Sunday *Script* it was. One I picked off of a load. Anybody throwed it out?"

No one had. Presently he was seated in the rocker, Elvie held against him with one hand, the other holding the Sunday magazine away from the child's fluttering fingers. Sitting on the floor, Florette listened intently.

" 'Boo-bonic pla-gue,' " Pop read slowly, moving the paper back and forth and squinting.

Coral twitched it from his grasp. "Oh, let me read it, Pop. You need glasses," she had the grace to add. " 'Bubonic plague has been found within reach of our cities, the same plague that ravaged the Middle Ages — ' That was way back when, Florrie — 'when thousands of people died in London alone, and were thrown into pits and covered quickly, not to spread the disease any more.' "

41

She went on to read of the discovery of it on our western prairies some twenty years ago, with only a few human beings known to be infected. Wherever it was found, the article continued, the Board of Health sprayed the animal burrows to kill the fleas, since the great danger was that infected fleas would bite rats, and the rats in turn would bite human beings. It was conceivable that a real epidemic could be started that way. Dumps, she read, her voice bitter at each repetition of the word, must be carefully supervised to be kept sanitary.

"Dumps," Pop gloomed, pulling a rag of handkerchief from his overalls pocket and wiping Elvie's mouth. "Dumps. They got just one idea, them big bugs: make it tough for the haulers. Know what they done now? Purt' nigh doubled the dumping fee us haulers has to pay. Gets much worse, they won't be no profit in it."

"But, Pop, one thing sure: we got to have a good, tight fence for Elvie," Florette urged.

"Ever occur to you that fences costs money?"

"That reminds me," Coral put in, laying down the magazine. "We got to have money for our schoolbooks, Pop. In this state they have a fee. And we have to get gym suits, too."

Pop's sigh wheezed through his whole body. "I figger what I've took in this far won't hardly buy us vittles for the next few days. If I can find me a store that will let us run a bill, why maybe I can squeeze out enough for the books. But looks like you got to go to gym in your jeans. We're scraping bottom for sure. And at that I been h'isting some mighty heavy trash." He put his hand to his back and wrinkled his nose as if in pain. "Yeah, I sure wisht you was a boy, Florrie."

"If you could maybe take some of the heavy jobs after schooltime, Pop — Even if I'm nothing but a girl I could sure help lug. But this prairie dog. The paper said about telling the Health folks. How would you go about it?"

"Whyn't you ask your teacher?" Pop suggested.

"Coral, you ask. I get so scared I don't know what to say."

Coral's frown was calculating. "Okay. I'll say we saw a sick prairie dog on a dump. Don't have to tell them we're on the dump ourselves. What business is it of theirs?"

The Board of Health took prompt action when the counselor reported the case. Its men sprayed all around the dump, and examined the prairie dog. Pop had buried it when he found it dead, and he unearthed it for them. "Reckon they caught some other critters, too," he said.

The school presented the matter at a special assembly. Fortunately the Board of Health had found no infected fleas in the area, but they advised everyone to avoid animals that could carry the plague.

Bubonic plague was not the only threat, the principal

explained. Many animals were afflicted with rabies. The newspapers now and then told of bats which bit the children who picked them up, and likewise skunks and raccoons which proved dangerous pets. Any sick or disabled wild animal should be especially avoided, and whoever noticed one should notify the Board of Health. Then the suspected animal would be kept confined until the necessary tests had been made. If the tests were positive, anyone who had handled the animal, even though not bitten, must undergo treatments that were long and painful, but not nearly so painful as the rabies which they prevented, and which caused death.

Coral was asked to tell the assembly just how the prairie dog had acted, and she stepped daintily to the platform and described it in her company voice. After school a dozen girls clustered around her, and she sauntered along with them while Florette loped away toward home. Looking back, she saw her sister getting into a funny little snubnosed car which barely held three girls.

When Coral came home, Florette asked her about the little car.

"Oh, the little Isotta. You open the whole front to get in. Belongs to a girl named Jane Brown. She took me to her house. Swell house," she added discontentedly. "Two bathrooms and a half."

"Whyn't this Jane fetch you home?" Florette eyed her sister suspiciously.

44

"Heavens and earth, think I'd let her? Like I said, I'd die of shame. I told her the doctor wanted me to walk every day. So I made her let me out before we came in sight of the place."

Florette let the subject drop there. She was thinking of animals and Elvie. "Pop," she said that night, her voice and body tense with resolve, "with Elvie so crazy for animals, we plain got to fence him in."

Pop took another forkful of beans, crossing his eyes at them with marked lack of relish. Beans were cheap, and when Florette had any say about it they were making a large part of the Cochrane menu. "Fencing is out right now, and that's flat," he growled. "But I hauled a playpen this very day, and I reckon I can fix it up for him. That way the little tyke can be outdoors and nothing can get at him."

Florette spatted Elvie's waving hands together. "He won't like it nearly so well. Will you, Florrie's angel?"

"Well, then, Florrie's angel can just lump it," Pop said severely.

"I should certainly think we could do without a fence until we can get a car and such as that," Coral said. "And talk about building on to this house, you haven't even nailed a board over the hole in the porch floor. I practically broke my leg there today."

"Nag, nag, nag." Pop stamped out, slamming the door so hard that the house shook. In another minute they heard his truck chatter and roar into action.

"Now look what you girls done," Mom sighed. "You know well and good what's likely to happen now."

"He isn't usually so crabby before he gets to drinking," Florette thought aloud. "You reckon he's feeling real bad, Mom? Seems like I'd ought to help him more. But I need more time for my homework, too."

"He ain't the only one feels bad." Mom was always ailing. "Seems like one of you great girls could give me a lift with my chores once in a while."

Coral sniffed. "What's the big idea, wasting time on a place like this? And I sure don't feel too good either."

Both girls studied the crowded room, to which Pop was always bringing sad pieces of furniture. Dusty. Dingy. Drab. And every room belonging to everybody. Not a corner where she could go to be quiet. Not a decent place to study: only the kitchen table, left partly set, with a light bulb dangling over it and making the letters even more confusing. Florette wondered whether she would do any better if she had a place for studying. The farmhouse hadn't offered much more space.

All in all, school was more difficult than ever. In Nebraska her teachers had learned what to expect of her. It was as if they passed the word along, shrugging their shoulders and saying, "What's the use of wasting time on her?" She would have dropped out long ago if it hadn't been for Pop. At any mention of her stopping, Pop's jaw would stiffen and he would say, "No sir. No

46

kid of mine is going without an education. Except poor little Elvie, of course."

Coral had always sailed along, never getting high grades, but never near failing. She was following the same program at Kennedy. She had friends, too. From a distance Florette could see her chattering with other girls, sometimes with Jane Brown, the one with the funny snubnosed car. Florette would have liked to know Jane. She was always scrubbed-looking, with starchy clean clothes and the snowiest oxfords Florette had ever seen outside a shoe department.

And boys hung around Coral. They seemed to bat remarks to and fro like Ping-pong balls, Coral as quick and easy as the others. Not that the remarks made sense, when Florette came near enough to hear them.

She herself spent her spare time in her homeroom, going over her books or just sitting. Those books! Always most of the little kids could read off the lessons as easy as anything, while Florette struggled in the thicket of letters, hardly able to make head or tail of them. Occasionally she tried so fiercely that the fight left her feeling sick and dizzy, but usually she didn't try.

In the beginning her homeroom teacher, Miss Sansome, had treated her like anyone else, but when the first two weeks had passed, her manner changed. First she was crisp and cool, and then Florette would feel the teacher's gray eyes upon her and would read in them a mixture of puzzled questioning, as if she were looking for something that wasn't there.

One day she stopped her as the class filed out. "Florette, can't you try a little harder? Your English teacher says you're not keeping up at all."

"Seems like I do try, Miss Sansome," Florette mumbled.

"It isn't your eyes? You had examinations at the school where you were before, didn't you?"

"Yes'm. They always said my eyes was okay."

Miss Sansome sighed. "Well, you'd better hurry and get into your gym suit," she said, and went back to her work.

Gym was different. First there was the gym suit. When Pop couldn't scrape up the money for books and suits, the teacher said cheerfully that there were always some suits left by students going on to high school. She found two, garments that were brand-new-looking, and exactly like all the rest.

Undressing, Florette laid her clothes in a careful pile, hiding ragged underwear under her dress, and then stepped happily into the one-piece garment. Some of the girls complained about the color, which was almost orange. Florette loved it, and felt warm and happy when she looked at it. And the gym teacher said, "My, but that color's becoming to you, Florette."

And the showers were a delight: warm water just by turning a knob.

Besides, she was good in gym. Her strong young body was ready and able for anything it had to do, and she was the equal of anyone and better than most. It was a wonderful feeling, but much too brief, and gym was only three times a week.

In many ways Home Ec also was easy. Florette had helped Mom with the house chores as long as she had helped Pop outside. It was kind of funny to make such little dabs of cookies or cake, measuring out the ingredients as if they were pure gold, but she was all right as long as she could do what the girl next her was doing, and didn't have to figure it out from a book. And it might be nice to know the fussy rules about setting a table, in case the Cochranes should sometime have company to supper.

Her third happy course was Art. Her drawings were queer, but since drawing was done as an expression of individuality, much of the class produced astonishing specimens. "And your color sense is unusual, Florette," the teacher said. "Unusually good."

6

Pop continued out of sorts. Florette helped him all she could, lifting tree branches and old metal and heavy boxes into the truck. It was not wholly disagreeable work, for Pop's loads were sometimes varied and interesting, and the dump itself held a sort of fascination, so that she wondered, every time they drove up to it, just what she would see there.

Certain haulers made a specialty of gathering up all the metal that was brought in, and selling it for scrap. Others sorted out the rags that could be sold to companies that did nothing but process them for sale as cleaning cloths. Still others watched for clothing that was good enough for the secondhand stores in Denver. You had to have a strong stomach, Florette thought, to hunt amid all the ugly sights and smells, yet there was a kind of adventure about it. You might even find a diamond ring. Or a whole doll for Elvie.

On one trip they saw a woman down in a dusky little cavern, fingering through a mass of clothing with her gloved hands.

"Whatever's that one after, in her million-dollar pants and sweater?" Pop asked one of the other haulers.

The other hauler made a scornful face. "Buttons! I seen plenty who come looking for old bottles — the ones that have turned kinda purple in the sun — but this is the first one after buttons. Seems like they collect buttons nowadays. She says she's found some jimdandies on town dumps. Well, it sure takes all kinds."

Florette's attention left the astonishing lady and returned to the treasure which she herself had found in one of their loads, and piled up carefully in the cab. One of their clients, as Pop liked to call them, had evidently cleaned out his garage, and among the discards were a dozen paint cans, which Florette knew by their weight were not entirely empty. Investigating them when they reached home, she sucked in her breath with pleasure. One held enamel almost the color of her gym suit, and several others contained a little white paint that had not dried past using. There were even stubby brushes and a half bottle of turpentine.

"Pop," said Florette, "I'm gong to start painting the house. Maybe after I've used up this white you can buy enough to finish it."

She spent a happy Saturday morning, splashing whiteness on those scaly weathered boards. She had difficulty deciding where to begin. Maybe if she started in front, where everyone could see it, the contrast would make Pop hurry to get more, but you couldn't count on that. Reluctantly she began at the back, where the patches would not be so noticeable. By using every

51

bit of the paint and turpentine, stretching it as far as she could — and painting fast — she covered almost half of that wall.

Pop watched her, sitting on his heels, arms wrapped round his knees. "Look at how the wood soaks it up. Like a plumb dry field soaking in the rain. Two coats won't be none too much. It's lucky you're through for now. I got a big hauling job this afternoon. Lady with an apartment house has a couple tenants moved out, and seems like they left a slew of stuff behind. Whole load. Need you to help h'ist, Florrie. This back of mine's purt' nigh getting the best of me."

Pop's loads were often interesting, and this afternoon's especially so. One thing was a tall old typewriter, and with it a large book, its back broken and its leaves dogeared.

"What's it say on the cover?" Florette asked her father.

"Tough typewriting lessons," he told her, scrutinizing it.

"What you mean, tough?" Coral jeered. It's touch —don't you see?—touch."

"Don't make any more sense that way," said Florette.

More immediately interesting were a few framed pictures, one of them in colors that made Florette feel as the gym suit and the orange enamel did. After the hours of lifting miscellaneous objects into the truck, and then emptying the useless ones on the dump, Florette still had energy enough to set up two or three of the pictures where she could look at them. She turned from them to the old machine again, fingering the keys, beautifully shaped and resembling ivory, and running a finger over the gilt letters on the body of the machine. "R-E-V-I-L-O," she spelled out. "Must be its name."

Coral jumped up from the couch where she had lain reading an old movie magazine. "You think that's funny," she snapped, "forever spelling things hindside before. After a while a joke wears out."

"Well, what does it say?" Florette asked, staring at the letters.

"Oliver. Natch. How anybody can be so dumb —"

"Pop, you reckon you could tinker it up so's it would work?" Florette brushed off her sister's scolding as a pony might brush off a fly, though her eyes flickered angrily toward Coral, as if the pony could kick and bite.

"Ain't much I can't tinker," Pop agreed. "But give a feller time, Florrie, give a feller time."

"Look, Corrie," said Florette, "this picture of sunflowers will hide the place in our room where the plaster's busted. And I think this orange paint would cover anyways the inside of our door and around the window. Wouldn't it kind of brighten things up?"

Coral was peering into skillets on the stove, where potatoes were frying and wieners boiling. "It would take more than some ugly orange paint to do anything for that hole," she scoffed. "Mom, can't we ever have anything besides wieners and spuds?"

"If you want something fancy, whyn't you fix some-

53

thing fancy?" Mom inquired sourly. With Elvie asleep on her lap she was rocking slowly and fingering through another backless magazine.

"Know what? I'm going to slap on that orange paint right now. Tonight," Florette said.

"You might anyways set the table for supper," Mom complained.

Florette did so with speed, and Coral snorted. "Sure like to have the Home Ec teacher see you. Knives and forks all in a heap that way."

"Do it yourself, then," Florette snapped back.

Coral shrugged. "Tin knives and forks and oilcloth with all the pattern worn off. Where's the use?"

Florette was already outside, vigorously stirring the orange enamel with a stick. She had soon spread the color over the inside of their door, as planned, but it had run out when half the window frame was covered.

She pounded in a nail and hung the yellow sunflower picture, and sat on her mattress — still without a bedstead — surveying picture and door with partial satisfaction.

Pop slouched in to see what she had done. "Reckon it won't be too long before I can scrape up money for the outside paint," he said. "This here room looks patched up, all right. Whyn't you finish off the window with a dab of that real bright blue they was in one of them cans? And we maybe could find some green to go around that baseboard. Then you could make out you was copying a patchwork quilt." He drew down his upper lip in his own particular grin.

"Oh, Pop, do you really mean it? About the house paint? You think we can really buy the paint?"

"We-ell, seems that way now," he drawled. "But look, kid, you better hyper in and get you some vittles before your mom or Corrie clears 'em out."

Florette would have liked to jump up and hug him, but he would have thought she was out of her mind.

It was only the next week — like in a TV movie, Florette meditated — that Pop came home with a long machine trundling behind his truck. Florette had just got home from school, and ran toward him, full of questions.

"This don't look like no junk," she said. "Whatever is it, Pop?"

He clambered from his seat and stood beside her, arms akimbo, looking at the strange object. His blue eyes were bright and his thin-skinned face flushed, so that Florette sniffed suspiciously. She could detect no alcohol aroma.

"What is it, do you ask? It's a surefire moneymaker, Florrie. Your pop's branching out in business. Just take a good look at this baby that's going to put us on Easy Street, practically. Put you in mind of anything?"

"Well, it does look like farm machinery, but nothing we ever had."

"A baler!" Pop laughed as at a great joke.

55

"But we got no hay."

In reply, Pop heaved from the truck a great brown bale, grimacing and grabbing at his back when he had put it down. "That's what it makes." His tone was triumphant. "Takes these here pasteboard boxes, mostly the kind with ridges in 'em. It chomps them up and squeezes 'em tight and fastens the bale neat and sure with the wire that feeds over this here spool at the side."

"But I don't see — "

"You will see, though. You'll laugh your head off when you get a look at the way it works. Mountains of boxes — " He waved a hand skyward — "and you feed 'em in here at this side. Then this critter rears up its head on its long jointed neck, showing its teeth for all the world like one of them dinnysours. And it comes down and butts the cardboard, and chomps it — "

"But what for?" Florette demanded.

"Money, that's what for. You load up a ton of them bales and cart them into Denver to them big paper dealers. They put acid on 'em and let it work to where they can make it into new pasteboard. No end to it. Big sale. Lots of money."

"But what did you have to pay for it?" Florette recalled the prices of the farm machinery Pop hadn't been able to buy.

"They was real reasonable. Took what I had on me for the down payment. Then I pay the rest on time, out of what this baby makes for me. Don't cost me nothing, in a way of speaking."

The paint money —

"What you figure to do with this baler, mister?" a man's voice broke in. It was one of their neighbors, a half block away. Florette had noticed his house, because it boasted both paint and fence.

Pop tilted his cap farther back and scratched his head, his face benevolent. "Figuring to make me a good chunk of money with it."

"Jake Riddle, other side of the dump, he unloaded it on you, didn't he?"

Pop's grin stiffened. "How you mean, unloaded it?"

The neighbor cackled. "That Jake. Sure a cool customer. Only for once he got took, same as you. Thought he was going to get rich with this here contraption."

"But it works real neat." Pop's voice thinned and cracked. "I seen it deliver the goods. And it ain't in bad shape. Hardly been used. And it wasn't no Jake. They said at the shop it was a feller that left town." Pop seemed to be pleading his case in a courtroom.

The caller, John Nelson he said his name was, cackled anew. "Why shouldn't it be in good shape? Before the dollars began to roll out of it, the whole neighborhood turned to and clapped an injunction on Jake. He had to shut up shop before he'd opened it."

"But why? Good gravy, why?"

"Because this ain't no industrial zone." Mr. Nelson's sweep of arm took in crouching houses and acres of prairie.

"Zone? How do you mean zone?"

"Barnett's getting real newfangled. We're inside city limits, right up to the dump we are, though you might not guess it till you got your tax bill. And they zoned the town, and this here is residential. A business like this baling is prohibited. Lower the value of our property."

"You mean I can't use this machine, now I got it?"

"That's right. Hope you didn't pay out much money on it." John Nelson's eyes appraised the house as he spoke.

Pop kicked the baler. "Mister, you wouldn't be kidding?"

The neighbor shook his head. "Didn't know you was the one Jake picked to be the fall guy. But the fellows around here have been ready to run to City Hall quick as anyone tried to get into the business."

"Seems like somebody could have been friendly enough to warn a fellow," Pop protested.

Florette did not wait to hear the man's answer, for Mom was calling to her, and she was glad to escape before her wrathful tears overflowed. She loathed tears.

Explaining the unlucky transaction to Mom, Florette, with her habitual gesture, picked Elvie from the floor, where he was crying from the splinters he had managed to collect. Straddling him across her hip she gave little mechanical jumps and jounces to amuse him.

"Your pop's not got the business sense of a grasshopper!"

"You've no call to fault him like that," Florette retorted, her anger transferring itself at once. "Pop's a farmer, and a good farmer, if only the big rich farms — "

"Well, seems like you'd go help him," Mom scolded in her turn. "He ain't got the back for h'isting them bales."

Florette thrust Elvie at her mother and ran. Mr. Nelson was halfway home, and Pop was grunting and straining as he heaved the bales out of the truck. He slumped against the tailboard, gulping the air and mopping his wet face with the aging bandanna.

Next morning he pulled the quilts higher and said he didn't aim to get up. He felt right poorly. Mom buttoned a sweater over her nightgown, shuffled out to the kitchen, and put on the kettle to boil for coffee.

When Florette, hurriedly dressing, took him a hot cupful, he shook his head. "You and your mom don't never get the hang of making decent coffee."

They all thought Pop was sick because of losing his down payment and his dreams of profit, but it might be partly because he had strained his back again, lifting the ill-fated bales without help. Yes, his back was sure bad, he grunted. It was that sacred iliac of his, and what there was sacred about it, blamed if he knew.

When Florette laid an unaccustomed hand on his

59

forehead, high and white where it had been kept from sunburn by his cap and his waving hair, she found it disturbingly hot.

"Pop, you're burning," she cried. "Mercy to us, you got a real fever."

"You're telling me. But quick as I throw off these blasted covers, it's like you was slopping ice water over me."

"There's a lot of kids out of school with some kind of flu," Florette commented. "Looks like you ought to take aspirin."

Mom said they were fresh out of aspirin, and there wasn't a smidgin of Mentholatum or such as that.

"Lard and turpentine," Pop snarled. "Any fool knows lard and turpentine. But it sure is a pity you ain't bothered to get you your driver's license, Florrie" — his bloodshot eyes glared at her — "so's you could go to the drugstore after some aspirin."

"I'll go and get the last drops of turpentine," Florette apologized.

When Coral woke next morning with the same sort of fever and hoarseness they were all sure it was flu in both cases, though Pop's was aggravated by disappointment and a strained back. That back would not even let him sit up. "Grabs a feller like it hates him and wants to shake the bejabers out of him," he said in one of his better moods.

Florette walked to the nearest drugstore and got aspirin for both patients, being unable to coax another

drop of turpentine out of the old cans. Pop was better
the third day, when Coral's misery was deepest.
Florette did not go to school either. For one thing,
Mom was on the verge of the same sickness.

"To hear you tell it," Pop grumbled, "nobody can't
get nothing without you get it worse. I'm surprised you
ain't got the sacred iliac before this."

Mom rocked and sighed and murmured that if some
folks had the back she'd had ever since little Elvie was
born, she guessed they'd think the sacred iliac was as
pretty as it sounded.

Anyway, Florette couldn't leave Elvie without someone who would be more responsible for him. Likely
Mom really wasn't too well, and, cooped up in the stuffy
little house, she kept falling asleep in her chair.

On Pop's fourth day he was slouched in the rocking
chair from the dump, the one with a brick piecing out
its broken leg, so that sitting must be carefully accom-
plished. He was listening to a radio program, and
Florette surprised a dreamy expression on his face.

Coral did not notice her father's expression, but she
did notice the program, and jerked erect where she lay
on the swaybacked sofa, with one of the everlasting
movie magazines. You could always find someone on
the sofa and someone in a rocking chair, Florette
thought.

"Good heavens, Pop!" Coral cried. "Can't we have
anything but that old farm hour? Who wants to hear
the price of wheat and hogs and eggs?"

Pop made no move to change the station. "That Chuck Miller. He's got such a folksy way with him. Anything he says sounds good."

Pop just couldn't admit that he was lonesome for the farm, lonesome as all get out.

Coral dropped back with a squall of springs and lay glaring at Pop and the radio, and then at Florette and through their doorway at the sunflower picture and the orange on the window frame.

"You look awful uncomfortable, Corrie," Florette said, regarding her flushed face and tumbled hair. "Whyn't you take you a nice bath and comb your head? Look, I'll smooth up your bed while you're doing it, and maybe you'd catch a nap."

"Bath!" Coral exploded. "You take notice how Mom's got dirty clothes soaking in the tubs?"

Florette whipped the sheets and quilts into place with a cross jerk. She had forgotten that this was one of the times when Mom had let the wash accumulate because the pump was so crotchety that getting enough water was a job in itself, and the supply of coal and wood so low that heating it was another problem. That was why the floor looked a shade worse than usual. And with the floor so dirty it hadn't seemed worth while to pick things up and make the place tidy.

"I'll go to bed though," Coral said, flouncing off the sofa and into the girls' room, and dropping down on her pallet. "At least I can cover my ears and not have to hear any more about canners and cutters."

At that precise moment the Cochranes heard a tapping at the door. It was so unusual that Coral sat up and she and Florette both peered toward the window. At what they saw, Coral flopped down again, jerked the covers up to her chin, and whispered, "Oh, no! That's Jane Brown's car out front. Do something, somebody. I'll die —"

In the sitting-room Pop was already saying, "Come in, come in. Scuse it if I don't get up, young lady. Got a misery in my back. You looking for somebody?"

"I must have got the wrong place." Yes, it was Jane's voice, deeper than most girls'. "I'm sorry to have bothered you. It must have been Jasmine Street after all."

The sisters were holding their breath, and Coral kept her eyes squeezed shut while her lips were silently saying, "Oh, go, go, go!"

Both let out their breath when they heard Jane's quick tread across the porch. Then it paused, and she seemed to be turning as she said, "I was looking for Coral Cochrane. Would you have any idea — ? At the office they said she lived on Jasmine. The family moved to Barnett only this spring."

Coral flattened on the mattress when Pop's chair thumped down and Pop's voice said warmly, "Why, no, we don't live on Jasmine, young lady. We live right here. Ain't had time to get it fixed up yet," he added hastily. "But Coral's my girl all right. Come in, come in."

For once Florette thought she could feel just what Coral was feeling. The front door creaked wider open, and Jane's steps hesitated across the sitting room, evidently following Pop's motioning hand.

"Florrie — do something!" Coral begged.

But already Jane stood looking in at them with puzzled eyes. For a long moment nobody said a word. Then Pop limped up behind Jane, with a hand on his back, and remonstrated, "Cat got your tongues, Corrie? Florrie? Whyn't you mind your manners and ask the young lady to come in?"

As he spoke he reached past her and tilted a chair to slide from it Elvie's stuffed rabbit and a huddle of Coral's clothes. With a breathless thank-you Jane perched on the edge of it.

"I'm so sorry you're sick, Coral," she stammered. "Lots of the kids have been out, but with both you and your cousin — it's been four days now, so I was worried about you — "

"How did you find us?" Coral demanded hoarsely.

"Well — " Jane hesitated. "I went to a Jasmine address they gave me at the office, but it was an old couple. The secretary must have got it mixed up — "

Coral's voice was at once harsh and limp. "But how did you find this — this dump?"

"There was a girl walking along Jasmine who thought she'd seen you here — "

"I suppose it would have had to come out sooner or later," Coral muttered. She slid an estimating glance at

Florette and lowered her voice. "This isn't what I'm accustomed to, Jane. My uncle and aunt were the only relations I had left when my — my own parents were killed in a — in an airplane crash. After I've finished my education, and when I'm of age, I can get away, but now — "

As if involuntarily, Jane's clear hazel eyes traveled round the room. Florette seemed to be seeing it with those eyes, and it was suddenly much worse. Of course she had known it was bad, but it was like trying to sweep a muddy road clean to make any headway with it. Oh, if only she had scoured the floor again, and picked up the odds and ends that cluttered every available space. Trashy, that was the only word for it: trashy.

There was another silence, finally broken by the caller: "I see you're painting your woodwork. That's a nice color. And the picture" — she was looking at the sunflowers — "it's one of my favorites."

"You kidding?" Coral asked incredulously. "Plain old sunflowers? Plain old vase, too, and not even drawn straight — "

Jane laughed as if Coral were joking. "Yes, the Van Gogh. That's a nice print of it. I've got one in my room, too, but not such a good reproduction."

Out of another overstretched silence Jane stirred and rose. "Well, I hope you'll soon be back at school, Coral." She was almost stuttering. "Your cousin, too. I expect I better be running along. This flu is pretty contagious."

65

7

Silence tightened over the Cochrane house until the snubnosed red car had spun away. Florette thought Jane herself was upset, for at first her motor chattered and whined and refused to take hold. "Flooded it," Florette muttered.

Still the silence held the three Cochranes. It was broken when Mom came yawning out of her bedroom, with Elvie clasped across her middle.

"Peddler?" she asked, the word distorted by another yawn. "Agent?"

Pop's feet banged down and he glared at her and at Coral. "Naw, one of Coral's fine-feathered friends. You'd ought to have been here, Mom. You'd have learned something. Did you ever guess we was Coral's uncle and auntie? Don't it look to you like a niece better rustle her stumps and earn her own living?"

Coral's only comment was a sniffling wail.

"That ain't no answer, my fine young lady," Pop growled. Hitching himself to his feet, he pulled on his peaked cap and strode from the house.

Mom complained, "Now you done it, whatever it is you done, Coral Cochrane."

Florette pressed her face to the window and watched the truck head straight for a little building set close to the street and topheavy with a huge sign: LIQUOR.

"I sure hope they don't give him much credit," Mom grumbled. "Phone bill due before we know it, and the electric. Looks as if when he's so bad lamed and so worried-like, you girls would keep out of his hair. I don't get the straight of it, Corrie. Who was it come to the door? And what was all that about uncles and aunts?"

Coral choked on her tears. "Oh, Mom, for Pete's sake can't you skip it?"

"Corrie was just kind of kidding, Mom," Florette said, carrying Elvie off for a change and a washing of face and hands. Again she was seeing through Jane's clear eyes, and she shuddered. Elvie was a beautiful baby, but she couldn't imagine him pressed up against Jane's immaculate sweater. And Mom — Mom had a kind of pretty face, even if she was crowding forty, but she had let herself go — how she had let herself go!

Florette rummaged through the dresser drawers in her parents' bedroom. "Hasn't this poor tyke a clean dud to his name?" she asked, disgust rasping her voice.

It was suppertime before Pop returned, walking carefully and scowling. Even Elvie scuttled out of his way, and the woman and the girls asked no questions and made no comments.

Pop showed his teeth at the dry chips of hamburger on the stove, and flung away into the bedroom to subside into heavy sleep. He hardly stirred from the room until the next afternoon.

Florette had just come in with her schoolbooks, letting a breath of fresh air into the close-smelling house. In her old bathrobe, Coral sat slumped before the TV, viewing it with dull eyes.

"Whyn't you been to school, niece, like your cousin?" Pop demanded.

"Oh, Pop, can't you let me alone? I don't feel so good. And I don't want to go back to that old school again — not ever!"

Pop grabbed the nearest chair and whanged it to the floor in a splintered mass. "By rights I'd ought to take a good stout belt to you, Coral Cochrane," he gritted between his teeth. "Think you're above the rest of us, and don't hardly turn a hand to help me and Mom. But school's one thing I won't budge about. You got to go if I have to lick you the whole way there."

Coral was rocking herself to and fro almost as her mother sometimes did, and the tears crept under her lowered lashes. "Oh, I wish I was dead," she moaned. "I wish I'd never been born."

Next morning Pop was still a thundercloud, and the family kept out of his way as far as the crowded house would let them. Coral didn't get up for breakfast, and when Pop had eaten some bread and drunk several cups of bitter coffee, he limped to the door and glowered down at the back of her head, which was all that showed above the huddled covers.

68

"Niece," he roared, "shake a leg and get ready for school. No excuses, now. Not a word out of you."

Breathing gusty remonstrances, Coral flounced from among the quilts, keeping herself as far from her father as possible, slammed the door and dressed.

It was so late that she could stop only to swallow a cup of coffee. Both girls scuttled away, with glances at Pop and at the clock, which was notably unreliable.

"I don't give a hang if we're late," Coral gasped, slowing from the run with which she had started. "If we're late, the whole gang won't be lined up to see us come, that's sure."

"Why would they be lined up to see us come?"

"Well, figure it out for yourself. What that stuck-up Jane Brown will have told them!" Coral shook her head so furiously that she dashed bright tears from her eyes. "Can't you just hear her dishing it out to her gang?"

Though the thought struck at the pit of Florette's stomach, she spoke stoutly. "I don't think Jane Brown would do us that way. It's plenty bad to have had her see us like — like that. But I don't think she'd ever —"

Coral hooted. "Well, you sure got another think coming. Gosh, Florrie, I rather die than go back to that school. And I really don't feel good — "

"You're hungry," Florette said. "Didn't eat much for supper and nothing for breakfast. Good I made san'-wiches with the hamburger we left last night." She broke off, eyes empty of everything but consternation. "Corrie, we never brought our lunch along. We were so kind of stirred up. I left it there, in two paper bags, like always, on the kitchen table."

"It might be a good excuse for going back. And then it would be too late to come today."

Florette shook her head. "I wouldn't put it past Pop to take his belt to us if we tried anything like that. And I remember oncet or twicet he fetched us our lunch when we forgot it."

Coral drew a sharp breath. "Oh, I sure hope not."

"He will maybe feel he went too strong. Pop ain't mean at heart," Florette argued. "He might just take that way to make up for some of the things he said."

"He's still too mad," Coral said hopefully.

But at noon, when Florette went to the front entry, not having a lunch or the money to buy one, she saw the old truck come lumbering up and stop before the school-house. She could tell that truck as far as she could see it, because Pop had used an old wooden sign, vivid red, to patch a break in its body. When Florette glanced behind her, wondering whether Coral was where she could see it, too, she caught a glimpse of her sister hastily drawing back out of sight.

The truck rattled to a stop before the school: not only the truck and Pop, but Mom beside him, in her characteristic pose of clutching Elvie on the perilous slope of her lap. Elvie had spied two things and was uttering weird cries of joy and flapping his arms. He had seen his favorite person, and he had seen a small white poodle that Miss Sansome was taking for a walk.

With another glance over her shoulder toward the spot where Coral had disappeared, Florette ran forward, pushing between boys and girls and past Miss Sansome and the puppy. Reaching up, she took Elvie in her arms and he aimed wet kisses at her face. After a moment, though, he wriggled around for another sight of the poodle, his mouth wide with eagerness.

Miss Sansome came to a halt, smiling at him. "The little boy loves puppies, doesn't he?" she commented to Florette.

"Oh, yes'm," Florette stammered. "He just goes out of his head over them."

"You know him?" Miss Sansome asked. "But of course you do. He loves you as much as he does the puppy."

"Oh, yes'm. He is my brother, Elvie." Florette was fumbling in her mind for her manners. "Excuse me, Miss Sansome: this is my mother. And my father."

During the introductions, Elvie passionately tried to throw himself out of his sister's arms, flapping wavering little hands toward the poodle.

"You mind if I let him pet her?" Miss Sansome asked, and lifted the ball of white curls so that the wildly waving hands could half enclose it. "No, Cherry Blossom!" Miss Sansome protested. "He may not want you to kiss him."

"Oh, he loves it. Look at him."

Elvie's eyes had closed in pure bliss as the puppy licked his face with an eager tongue. More than likely

71

he was finding remnants of jelly bread, Florette thought.

When at last she had boosted Elvie back on the maternal hillside, Pop reached over the two paper sacks of sandwiches, touched the peak of his cap to Miss Sansome, and drove off. The pup braced itself on twig-like legs and barked after that fascinating human being.

"Did you ever see anything sweeter? He's a darling little boy, your brother, Florette. Is it cerebral palsy?"

Florette moistened her lips, nodding. "That's the name the doctor called it, ma'am. He — he isn't a dummy, Elvie isn't. Pop and Mom think he can't never be no different — any different. But, honest, he's got sense. He laughs at the right places when I tell him stories, and — " Florette's face was puckered with eagerness to put his case.

Miss Sansome nodded her understanding, her eyes intent on Florette even while she stooped to caress Cherry Blossom. "Has a doctor seen him lately?"

(She looks at me different, Florette thought with a rush of gratitude. She's looking at me like I'm — like I'm a person.)

She shook her head in answer to the query. "Not right lately. Mom's scared to death they'll take him away from us. Mom loves him," she added defensively, "even if she don't see that he's got his own kind of sense."

"Many cerebral palsy children are as smart as the smartest," Miss Sansome agreed. "It's just that the

72

brain cells that control their muscles are damaged, and that affects their speech and everything else except their thinking."

"And there ain't a thing that can be done?" Florette's question answered itself, it was so sad and resigned.

"Oh, why do you say that, Florette? If their — you might call them their thinking cells — if those weren't damaged, they can be taught. Didn't you know that? They can be trained to walk, or anyway to go around in a wheelchair, and to do ever so many things that make life good. As for your Elvie, I shouldn't be surprised if he could be taught to read and write. Oh, Florette dear, didn't you know that?"

To Florette's surprise, Miss Sansome's voice shook as if she were near tears. Florette clapped her mouth shut, wondering if she had been looking as goofy as Elvie did when the puppy kissed him. Now a cold thought flattened her rush of joy.

She spoke huskily. "But that would take lots of money. And we — we got no money."

"Is your father out of work?"

"No'm, Pop's in business for himself." Florette spoke with some pride. "He's a trash hauler. But he kind of hurt his back, lifting, and he's been laid up with that and the flu. I help him all I can, but I can't take the truck out — got no license. Pop was a good farmer, Miss Sansome, but he couldn't make a go of it when all the other farms was worked with machines and getting bigger and bigger."

73

"Automation," Miss Sansome assented. "It's both problem and opportunity."

Florette had heard the word often, but never before anything good about it.

"As to your little brother, though, I know the state has a plan for handicapped children — and adults, too, for that matter. Under some conditions the state and the federal government together stand part of the cost. Or all of it, when that is necessary."

Florette began to feel dizzy again. Elvie reading? Elvie getting around by himself?

"Goodness, you'd better find your cousin and eat your lunch," Miss Sansome remembered, glancing at the paper bags which Florette had crushed tight against her breast. "But there's a man, a counselor, who comes here from the rehabilitation center. How will it be if I write and ask him to come and have a look at little Elvie? We oughtn't to get our hopes too high before we know what his condition really is."

Again Florette's whirling, soaring spirits took a nose dive. "Pop and Mom, they wouldn't let anybody take Elvie away."

"They wouldn't have to. If he proves to be what they call educable, there's a day school where you could take him every morning and bring him home every night. Now run along and eat your lunch — if there's anything left of it."

8

Reaching home that night, the girls found Pop's anger at Coral still simmering. His disfavor included Florette.

"I sure ain't up to hauling," he growled. "I never look for any help from Coral. But if you had any git up and go, Florrie, you'd have took that driver's exam as soon as we got here, and then you could of took over the route when I was off my feed. Swell driver like you, it's plumb foolishness not to be driving. And when there's only one kind of work a person's fit for, seems like she ought to be willing to do it."

Florette shivered. "I'm scared to death of the test. All those policemen and everything — "

"They ain't even police," Pop contradicted her, and turned his wrath on Coral. "Niece, what you aim to do to earn your board and keep? I don't feel no call to break my neck for a niece."

"Oh, Pop." Coral flounced out of the house and beyond the reach of his scolding.

"But about the driver's license I ain't joking, Florrie," he resumed. "I sure don't figure you out. You ain't a scare-cat about most things."

"There's stuff you have to read — big words — "
Florette's mouth was paper-dry at the thought.

"Good land, if your pop can read them, when he
never went no further than fifth grade — It was then
my old man said I'd had plenty book learning, and he
jerked me out to help on the farm. That's why I set my
stakes to see you girls through high school. Like I say,
Florrie, I can't figure you out. Most ways you ain't no
dummy. If you was like poor little Elvie — "

Hearing his name, Elvie flapped his arms and gurgled
till Florette, as usual, picked him up and hugged him.
Besides, he would make a good change of topic, a coun-
terirritant, even though Florette knew that Pop would
get back to the driver's exam sooner or later.

"Mrs. Sansome — my homeroom teacher — she
thinks maybe Elvie could be taught."

"Taught? That poor mite? Taught what?" Pop
scoffed. "Taught to blow his own nose, maybe?"

"To read and write, even." Florette spoke breathlessly, as if she were throwing a lighted giant cracker at
them, and might herself suffer from the explosion. "But
anyway to get around better, and take care of himself
and talk some."

"Read and write! Now I've heard everything," Pop
sputtered.

Florette persisted. "She says there's a school where
they train them. She says she can't tell for sure, but she
wouldn't be surprised if the thinking parts of his brain
were as good as anybody's."

76

"Tell for sure! She's darn right she can't tell for sure. Saw the poor kid for five minutes — took notice of him because she's one of them dog-crazy females and Elvie went out of his head over her itty bitty tweetie — "

"But she says she'll write to a man who knows all about it. And when he comes to see Elvie he can tell whether Elvie could go to school — "

Pop's fist banged on the table. "School! School! And what would a school like that cost, even if the poor kid could get any good of it, which I don't for a minute believe?"

Mom was crying, and now she grabbed Elvie and rocked to and fro with him while he joined his wails to hers. "They shan't never take my baby away. Don't cry, Elvie: Mom won't let them get you."

"He wouldn't be taken away any more than me and Coral are," Florette explained, with some difficulty restraining herself from trying to outshout them all, "she says it's a day school."

"And what would it cost?" Pop came in. "Besides its being a piece of fat-headed foolishness."

"She thinks — the state and the United States pay for it if his folks can't."

Pop wriggled his neck in momentary silence. "Did I understand you to say that this here high muckamuck would come to our house and look at our Elvie? You took a heap onto yourself, Florrie. I must say you took a heap onto yourself."

Coral had come back to listen to the argument.

"Florrie hasn't a speck of pride," she said spitefully. "Letting somebody else come poking into this pigsty."

"You tell that Mrs. Whatyoumaycallit there's nothing doing," Pop agreed. "Elvie's our kid, and we don't aim to let him get took away where maybe he wouldn't be treated right."

Florette gave up trying to explain the day school plan. She said, "Pop, seems like this is the law." She was making a grab at the law, and hoping that it would back her up in an emergency, for Pop's respect for it was well known, and his proudest boast was that no Cochrane had ever broken it. "So if this man wants to come, and the law says he's got the right to, why, we couldn't keep him from it. But it does look like we'd ought to get this place halfway clean before he comes, even if we got no money for paint and such."

Pop, still working his neck around in his collar, went on muttering about Florette and her know-it-all teacher and the nosy gov'ment man. He ended by saying that if Florette had her a driver's license him and her could soon pick up enough to buy paint.

As if invoked by his words, the telephone rang long and loud, and a woman's voice asked if Mr. Cochrane could call at once for a load of trash. Florette's reply quivered with regret. "I'm real sorry, but Mr. Cochrane's been poorly. Would tomorrow do? Oh, I'm real sorry."

"It had to be right off, so she said she'd call someone else." Florette did not look at her father as she reported.

She tried not to hear his angry snorting as she went at the job of picking up the odds and ends that littered that room and the others, all visible from it. Here was a ragged sweater which Pop had shrugged off and dropped on the floor, a pair of socks, shiny with wear, likewise discarded, a drift of tattered and yellowed magazines on the broken-backed sofa, Coral's underclothes, still lying in a ring in a corner of the bedroom, a handful of nuts and bolts Pop had left nested in a weary-looking dish towel on the table. Florette flew at them with motions that cracked like a whip, and put them away, though not always in much better places.

Then she strode into her room and Coral's, and spread up the rumpled masses of bedding.

After that, she stood with arms akimbo and surveyed the place. Not much use scrubbing right now. It would need it again, long before the Man could possibly come. But — "Mom," she said, "I bet there's time to do that wash and hang it out before dark, the days are getting so long."

Mom said, "Leave it on the lines overnight? Let some good-for-nothing come along and take his pick?"

"Who'd bother to swipe any of our duds? Except those two newest dresses of Coral's," she added, resentment of those dresses in her voice. She was already building a fire to heat water. When the buckets were over the blaze she dashed into the "bathroom" and began to sort the clothes overflowing the two round tin tubs.

On the back porch stood an old washing machine that Pop had salvaged and put into fair running order. It was as crotchety as the pump, but before Mom had lumbered out into the kitchen to get supper, Florette had put it to work, thumping like an ancient threshing machine. By the time the meal was over, she had poured in the rinse water she had been heating on the stove, and finished out a load, hanging it on the line before she went to bed. This was only a small part of the soiled clothes, but there hadn't been time, hot water, soap or clothespins for any more.

Florette had stuffed the unwashed remainder into a packing box, and had used a tub to take a cold bath. Her other underwear would be dry enough to put on in the morning.

She felt a little more respectable as she started for school next day, though the clothes on the line did not look as clear and bright as she had hoped. And the house was already accumulating more litter.

Reaching the school grounds, she found Miss Sansome in the parking lot with her car sticking out in the way while she vainly pushed pedals and spun the wheel.

Shyly Florette approached her. "You reckon I could help?" she ventured. When Miss Sansome looked surprised, she added, "I'm real used to autos."

Dubiously the teacher slid to the other end of the seat. Florette jumped in and busied her hands with pedals and wheel, head cocked and eyes intent as if listening. "I think —" She jumped out, lifted the hood, peered in. "Yes'm, a couple wires — " She reached in as she spoke, and her strong fingers turned and twisted something, while she blew the stray hair out of her eyes. "Now if you'll try it," she suggested.

Miss Sansome tried it and her effort was rewarded by a purposeful hum, while Florette met her astonished gaze with a pleased blink and pushed at her heavy hair with a crooked elbow.

"Why, Florette," stuttered Miss Sansome. "Why, Florette!"

"It wasn't nothing," Florette disclaimed, contemplating her greased and blackened hands. "Just a couple wires got crossed. I been fooling around Pop's trucks since I was knee-high to a grasshopper. I only wisht books come half as easy."

"Good gracious, what I wish is that machines were half as easy as books. And here you can find out what's wrong and fix it even before you're old enough to drive." Miss Sansome broke off, color staining her white skin as if she remembered how surprisingly old Florette really was. "Or do you drive?"

"I can drive okay," Florette said. "I've driven round the farm for years, and I got a learner's license in Nebraska. But I haven't got one here."

"Doesn't your father want you to get one?"

"Oh, yes, Pop — Pop won't give me any peace. Pop's kind of sick, and he wants I should drive the truck by myself when he's poorly."

"Well, then, why don't you?"

Florette was kneading one grease-blackened hand with the other, and her reply was almost inaudible. "I'm — too scared. The driving part I can do easy. It's all those other things we've got to know — "

Miss Sansome spoke briskly. "Why, Florette, don't be silly. For a girl who can tinker up a motor the way you just did, that test ought to be duck soup. But it's almost time for the bell. Better go and get those hands washed. And thanks a million."

That afternoon Miss Sansome told the homeroom that she had had the surprise of her life. One of their classmates had found out what was wrong with her little car and fixed it quick as a mechanic could. "It was Florette Cochrane," she announced, and they all turned unbelieving eyes on Florette.

"If only we had that vocational school started," she said, "the one the Coon Valley district has been talking about for years — can't you imagine what Florette could do in auto mechanics classes, or electricity, or something like that? She'd probably be A plus."

Her hazel eyes had lingered so thoughtfully on Florette's face that the girl stopped at her desk on the way out. "You said — a school where they'd teach things like machines?"

Miss Sansome made an expressive face. "It's still a dream. It was to open last fall, and they keep promising. They need to have a fire lighted under them."

"Seems as if that kind of school would be tops," said Florette.

It had been pleasant to be for a little while the center of admiring attention. Yet it was not all pleasure. In the hall a small boy put himself in her way, feet spread and arms akimbo, and surveyed her with round eyes.

"How come the routine about fixing old Sansome's car? How come you're only in seventh with us kids if you're so smart? It doesn't figure."

Others of her classmates gathered round them, staring as they awaited her answer. "How come?" their spokesman repeated. "Huh? How come?"

"Autos are easy," Florette mumbled, and pushed past them.

Another boy stopped her. He was one of the tallest in the school, and was in Coral's classes. From the first day Florette had noticed him, because he reminded her of Georgie. It was mostly the good straight look from his eyes — blue eyes — as if he was really seeing the person he was looking at. And his ears stuck out like Georgie's. But after the first time or two she couldn't find the resemblance again. His build was bigger and stronger, with broader shoulders, and his wheat-yellow hair was almost white on top, where the sun had bleached it. And he wasn't stranded on the edge like Georgie, but spang in the middle of everything.

"What's this about you being a whiz with autos?" Fred asked. "Girl, that's my line. How come a girl can do such a swell job at it? Hey! Don't rush off like that. I got to get at the straight of this — "

Florette was already racing away. She bumped into

83

people as she went, and smiled at them with unusual warmth, because it was so funny and so nice to have a boy like Fred Barlow look at her that way.

Next day she was still noticed by some of her schoolmates, who studied her with doubting wonder. She wished she could surprise her English teacher as much with a recitation as she had astonished everyone else by twiddling a few simple wires; but she did little better than usual. Her spirits had settled down like a Coke with the fizz gone by the time she came to the end of the school day and to her homeroom. As she was about to leave her desk at the closing bell, Miss Sansome waved a bright-colored booklet at her, and motioned her to wait.

When the others had flocked out, she came and laid the booklet on Florette's desk. Puzzled, the girl stared at the cover, with its cartoon of a gay little man in uniform.

"You read this, Florette. If you read it over and over till you have it by heart, you won't need to be afraid of that test." Miss Sansome's eyes sparkled and snapped with intensity, and she fixed them on Florette as if they were a pair of hands pulling her.

Florette moistened her lips. "Thank you, ma'am."

The teacher went back to her desk, and Florette slowly opened to the first page. Finger moving from letter to letter, she spelled out the words with silent lips: "If — you — are   a   res — res — of — Co-lo-ra-do — "

Intent though she was, she could feel Miss Sansome returning and hovering over her before Miss Sansome's hand came down on hers, and Miss Sansome's voice reproved, "I'm sure your teachers have told you, Florette. You mustn't use either your finger or your lips when you read to yourself. Do it with your eyes and mind only." She went back to her desk, leaving Florette to stare helplessly at the page.

Presently she got up and went to the teacher. "May I take the book home, Miss Sansome? If I am careful?"

"Why, certainly," Miss Sansome said.

As Florette emerged from school a pleasant thing happened. Jane Brown and Coral stood on the steps, and as Florette started past, Jane beckoned her to join them.

"Gooks, what a smart cousin you have," she said to Coral, who gave her an incredulous stare at the words. "Florette, one of the kids in your homeroom told me about your fixing Sansome's car. If that isn't something! We couldn't do it in a million years, could we, Coral? And we think we're the smart ones —" She broke off, flushing at her own slip.

"Hmph," said Coral.

"But I was just asking Coral," Jane hurried on, "if you two had started going to church here. Didn't I understand you to say you hadn't?"

Coral jerked her head in a curt negative. "No, not here."

"Well, we've got a keen class," Jane said, a hand on

each girl. "We have buzz sessions, where we discuss all kinds of junk — you'd be surprised: not a bit stuffy. And we have parties. It's a mixed boys' and girls' class," she added, giggling as if she knew the boy part would always matter most to Coral.

"Is it far off, your class?" Coral asked. "Pop — Uncle Jim — hasn't got his new car yet. He couldn't get the color he wanted, and has to wait. We haven't anything but a truck at present." She laughed and made a face. "You don't go to church in a truck."

"Oh, that." Jane dismissed the truck. "I'll be glad to pick you up. You can both crowd in, if you don't mind sitting on each other. Bucket seats."

"My cousin always takes care of Elvie," Coral hastened. "With my aunt so poorly. She says she needs Florrie Sundays, to get on her feet again," she elaborated.

"Oh, but just for an hour or two," Jane coaxed. "Florette, you can make it up to your mother some other way, can't you? You will come?"

If Coral had not given her a vicious pinch behind Jane's back, Florette would probably have refused. Stinging from those pointed nails, she said, "Thank you, I'll be glad to try it."

9

THAT DAY the sisters walked away from school together, Coral evidently aware of the uselessness of separating herself from Florette after Jane had publicly linked them. She said no word to her companion until they had passed all their schoolmates and were out on the open road.

"And just what do you think you're going to wear to that stuck-up Jane Brown's stuck-up church?" she demanded.

"You've got no call to say she's stuck-up." Florette defended Jane. "You said she wouldn't have no more to do with us after she saw where we lived, and look!"

"Yeah, look!" Coral mocked. "Makes me feel noble, that's how it makes her feel. But we weren't talking about that stuck-up Jane Brown. We were talking about what dress you think you'd wear. If you ever paid any attention to how you looked —"

Florette felt the hot blood surging to her forehead. "You know good and well, Coral Cochrane, that after you bought those two dresses for yourself there wasn't any money left for me and Elvie. Mom, either."

Coral tossed her head. "That's ancient history. The

87

fact remains: you haven't a rag fit to wear to church. If you know what's good for you, you'll make an excuse to Jane Brown tomorrow."

"I passed my word."

"Oh, your word! I tried to warn you not to say yes, but you're too dumb to take a hint."

The following days were busy ones for Florette. Pop was ailing too much to handle any but a few of the lightest hauling jobs. If he had taken in a fair amount of money Florette might have been able to get a new print dress. The cheap ones didn't look nice very long, but for the first few times —

Since no extra money came in, she had to pick out her best-looking dress, the one she wore to school, and make it as presentable as she could. She mended a rip she had hardly noticed before, and sewed on a button, and washed it with extra care, ironing it, though it did pretty well without. Polish covered most of the shabbiness of her shoes, and stockings were no problem, for her legs were so smooth and brown that nobody would notice that they were bare. Besides, even rich girls often went without stockings.

While she mended and ironed, Pop read aloud to her from the driver's examination book, and she tried to fasten some of the rules in her mind. "Rectangular — does that mean like a box?" she would ask, with lifted iron. "And octagonal — oh, my!"

"Eight-sided, dumbbell," Coral snapped, carefully flowing the scarlet enamel on her nails.

Pop spatted the instruction book shut. "You best hyper down there and take that test, Florrie. I'll drive you there after school tomorrow."

Florette shook her head, her eyes darting angrily around the room. "Pop, I can't do everything. Looks like you could anyway give me till next week to take that test. I got to scrub this floor and clean things if nobody else will. It's got to look nicer than this when Jane Brown picks us up Sunday morning. And looks like Coral has to spend hours every day on her fingernails and her hair. Hours and hours."

"Like enough Jane Brown won't take the trouble to come in," Coral sniffed. "Just honk at us from out front."

And that was what Jane did, after even Florette had begun to think that she had forgotten them.

"She's late," Coral said darkly. "Likely she's wishing she'd never asked us. What do you bet she won't show up at all?"

"She will too," Florette retorted, rubbing Elvie's face with a wet rag and then scrubbing at the jelly he had dribbled down his front.

"Well, if she shows up at all, it will be late enough so she can sneak us in without having to introduce us." Coral insisted.

Then came a triple beep from Jane's car and the sisters hurried out. Coral's floating hair glittered and her skirts swung and her heels clicked, while behind them clumped Florette's old oxfords.

Elvie rolled and scuttled to the door and sent a wailing cry after his First Lady, and Jane stuck her head up through the open top of the car and waved at him. Florette hoped she could see from that distance that he was clean, except for the faint remaining smear of jelly.

Plenty of people were still milling round the church when Jane drove into the parking lot behind it. Florette tried not to see them: small boys looking unnatural in suits and stiff white shirts and neckties; small girls twirling themselves into pompons of skirt and petticoat, some of them wearing doll-size white gloves; teen-age boys and girls exchanging banter; men calling genially to one another; women herding their children.

Jane did hurry through the crowd and to the church basement, where a small auditorium was filling with young people. "This is where our class assembles," she told her guests.

Sitting halfway back, Florette could observe ahead of her all the smart, immaculate clothes, could feel behind her all the eyes boring into her droopy old dress. She tried to turn her fingertips under and out of sight when Jane handed her a hymnbook. It seemed as if the nails were always grimy from tinkering with the truck, and the scrubbing of floors didn't quite remove the dark accumulation. She had tried some bleach that her mother used in the wash. Its odor still clung, but the dusky rims persisted.

She liked the singing, and was almost comfortable by the time they filed into the classroom. Class proved an ordeal.

Smilingly the teacher announced, "Jane has some new girls to introduce."

Jane, between the sisters, bounced up and pulled them to their feet. "This is Coral Cochrane," she said, nodding toward Coral, "and this is her cousin, Florette Cochrane."

Florette folded herself quickly into her chair while Coral smiled right and left.

The taking up of the collection was all right, for Florette had been hopefully putting away small coins toward the house paint, and she shared two nickels with Coral. It was the class reading of the lesson that terrified her, each member reading a verse aloud. As the boy next her finished his verse, Florette stared at the lesson paper with blurring eyes.

Coral cleared her throat and spoke in her best company voice. "You'll have to excuse my cousin. She has trouble with her eyes."

Starting so poorly for Florette, it was a difficult hour, and she had nothing to say as Jane drove home with them. Coral chattered, Florette had no idea about what.

But all Coral's gay lightness evaporated when the two were inside the house. "Oh, was I ever ashamed!" she said between clenched teeth, flinging to the floor the paper they had given her and stamping on it.

Florette spoke stonily. "I won't go again."

"I should hope not. Neither will I," Coral exploded.

Pop demanded, "Weren't they nice to you?"

"Real nice," Florette said wistfully.

"Grrrr, the way they looked at us —"

"A real nice old lady stopped me on the way out," Florette argued. "She asked me was I new in town and said she hoped I'd come again."

"Who cares about the old ladies?" Coral jeered. "And even most of the old ladies looked us up and down as bad as the young ones."

"I bet none of the girls was any prettier than you," Pop assured Coral. Pop and Mom were like Florette, they couldn't help being proud of Coral's flowerlike prettiness.

"The old ladies maybe thought you used too much lipstick," she said, scrutinizing her sister.

"Well, let 'em think. It's no skin off my nose." Coral lifted her little chin higher and studied the effect in the glass.

"Florrie," Pop asked uneasily, "you got no better dress than that one? It does look kind of strubbly for Sunday-go-to-meeting."

"Best I've got," Florette said shortly, noticing that she hadn't mended the rip very neatly, and that the button she had sewed on didn't match and stood out white and big.

"You ought to stick up for yourself or who will?"

Pop complained. "Didn't I give you girls money for a dress apiece, just before we left Nebrasky?"

"Coral found two that was real good bargains. Her size."

Coral was humming loudly enough not to hear their words as she inspected a small red spot on her chin.

"Anyhow," Pop accused, "there'd be money enough for a new dress if only you'd get that driver's license."

"We got to pay the telephone first," Mom put in.

"And the paint for the house," Florette reminded him.

As he often did, Pop defended himself with anger. "You got no call to complain, Florrie Cochrane, if you ain't willing to do your share, and put yourself out enough to take the driver's test. Looks like you're just plain stubborn. Drive as good as anyone, and won't bother to get yourself fixed up so's you can take out the truck alone." He was glaring at her, his thin face flushed. If he got any madder he'd be taking off to the liquor store and piling up bills they never could get paid, besides being cross as a bear.

"I'll go down this week," Florette promised. "I'll go tomorrow."

Pop's thunderclaps died away to rumbling. "One thing about you, Florrie," he admitted, "you don't make promises and then forget all about them. If you was to put in a couple hours hauling ever' day after school, and then Saturday mornings — Say, can't you just see

93

this little old house like a — like a snowball in its new paint? And the whole spit and bilin' of us in new clo'es — "

Pop's sun was shining again, but not Florette's. She picked Elvie up and carried him outdoors so they should not talk to her any more. She wished she didn't get so mad at every single one of them — Pop least, perhaps because he did admit that she was not wholly dumb. Almost, but not quite wholly. Could she, by some miracle, pass that terrible test? "God," she whispered, "couldn't you please give me a lift?"

Elvie clamored at her, pushing himself away to look into her pondering face.

10

AFTER DINNER that Sunday, when Elvie was safely asleep, Florette crouched under a window with the red and blue booklet, whispering the words as she pointed out their letters with a long, strong forefinger. She felt guilty to be whispering and pointing when Miss Sansome had told her it was practically a sin, but right now she had to help herself all she could.

Concentration was difficult, for Pop had the TV going and Coral the radio. There wasn't a spot in the house where Florette could get away from the medley of words, spoken and sung, to make any sense of the printed ones.

"My land!" Coral yelled at her. "Do you have to spell those words out loud?"

Florette was glad to have Elvie waken and give her a good excuse to stop struggling, put the booklet away out of his reach and take care of him.

"You know something?" she crooned, swinging him in her arms as in a hammock. "Maybe Elvie's going to school. Yes, and maybe he's going to read pretty books. Like this one — " She seized a fragment of picture book and sat down with him.

He was looking at her so blankly that she sighed. But then his attention focused on the pictures and she took heart. "We don't talk to you like you was a person, do we, baby? So how can you know the words? Do you suppose it's something like Sister and the words in the books? Now the pictures we both get. Look, Elvie. Here's a boy. He's a rich little boy. He's just as big as Elvie. And he has a dog. It's a white dog, a little like Miss Sansome's, the one that kissed Elvie with its tongue."

Elvie threw himself back against her breast and giggled until he choked.

"And this girl has a blue dress. Elvie say blue," she begged him, making her mouth kiss-shape for the letter b.

Elvie pushed his face close to the page and bubbled at the blue dress. Then he wavered his lips upward and blew toward the pictured sky. Florette caught her breath and, squeezing him tight, rocked him to and fro, laughing. "Elvie knows blue!" she cried. "Nobody can make me believe Elvie don't understand things."

Momentarily Coral turned off the radio. "Now what are you gabbling about?"

"I bet you most anything if a person knew how to go about it they could teach Elvie to talk."

"There you go," Coral snorted, switching on the sound again. "Next you'll be saying they could teach you to read good. Goofiest idea. Ought to have your head examined."

"Well, after the first those teachers never tried," Florette thought aloud. "So I didn't, either. But if I could somehow get hold of it right. Oh, I know Sister is slow as molasses, Elvie, and most ways awful dumb. But I can't help believing you and me both — All the same, I don't see a speck of use working on that auto book any more. Looks like it's just up to God. Or maybe if they'd let me drive first, and see how good I was at that —"

All night she dreamed restlessly, tossing and turning so much that twice she had to get out of the hot muddle of bedding, to smooth it up, and rearrange Elvie, and tuck the covers under at the foot.

"What ails you, Florrie?" Pop inquired next morning as she stood at the table, munching a bit of bread and gulping coffee. "You look like something the cat drug in." His eyebrows drew down over glittering eyes. "Now if it was Corrie I'd expect you to say you was sick and couldn't take the test today."

Florette shook her head, her mouth full.

"Want I would pick you up at school and take you down to the license place?"

Choking on the bread she hurried to swallow, Florette shook her head once more, and finally said, "I rather come home first, Pop."

Coming home first would put off the ordeal a little longer.

All that day she felt as if paralyzed by the trial ahead. When Miss Sansome asked, "Taken the exam yet, Florette?" she could hardly shape her stiff, dry lips to answer, "No'm. This afternoon."

"Well, good luck," the teacher lightly wished her.

Luck! What she needed was a miracle.

After school she started homeward so slowly that Coral overtook her even before they reached the farmhouse with the barking dogs. At home she washed her face, brushed her hair with the molting family hairbrush, retied her shoes more carefully, hiding a knot in the lace.

"My land," Pop protested, "never knew you to primp like this. Anybody'd think they was some nice-looking boy at the license place. All old men like your pop. Ready now?"

Dumbly she nodded and followed him out to the truck.

As they rattled over the outlying streets, Pop darted a suspicious glance at her. "What you mumbling about? They do say talking to yourself is a sure sign you're off your rocker."

"Just — just thinking." You couldn't tell Pop you were asking God if He wouldn't give you that lift. Pop didn't take much stock in God. *But if you'd anyway have them let me drive first off* —

Downtown before a neat office building Pop drew up and parked the car. "Here you are," he said jovially, "large as life."

She felt herself twice as large as that when she followed him in, her feet slapping the floor and her hands swinging as if they wanted to get away as badly as she did.

"I've fetched my girl to get her license," Pop said.

"Name? Age?" inquired a clerk, not an old man like Pop, but a starchy woman.

"You take this list of questions," she said, "and look them over. Then we'll have you give us the answers. Good gracious, girl, you're shaking like a leaf. Nobody's about to eat you. We'll give you the question part first, so you can get over shaking before one of the men takes you out in your car. Sort of ease you into it."

Ease her into it. Had God got the signals mixed?

She stumbled over to a desk where a boy was studying one of the same lists. Blindly she stared at hers.

"They take you over here," said Pop, pointing the way.

"Now I'll just ask you the questions. Miss Cochrane," said a uniformed attendant. "Come come, they're not so hard. Just take it easy. What do you need if you are to drive a vehicle in the State of Colorado?"

"A driver's license," Florette said breathlessly.

He laughed. "Well, sure. But what do you need to get the license?"

"You need to know — something about autos — and something about the laws —"

"Now these road signs," the man went on, nodding. "Look through this glass. What does that rectangular sign mean?"

99

Rec — rec — Where had the word gone? And how had it managed to take all Florette's thoughts with it? *Now, God, this is it. Please.*

"Go on, Florrie, for cat's sake."

"Take it easy, miss."

She managed to stumble through some of the signs. She recognized them out on the road, but here they looked different somehow.

"Now what do we mean when we say you need acuity of vision?"

Acuity of vision. Pop hadn't known what it meant, and when Florette tried to look it up in the school dictionary, the bell rang before she could decipher the small print. Now she shook her head.

But shaking her head seemed to shake every thought out of it. After another unanswered question or two, she stammered in despair, "Mister, I — I just got to study it some more."

Pop snorted, but the examiner's voice was kind. "You can try again tomorrow or a month from now, sister. But while you're here, why don't we let you try — "

He must mean to let her try driving. Her heart lifted at the thought, and Pop said, "Yes, you put her behind the wheel, and she'll sure show you something."

The attendant shook his head. "No use giving her the driving test until she's passed this part. But we may as well find out about that old acuity of vision, and see if she needs glasses. I didn't mark you off on that one,

100

sister. It looks like they could just as well have said sharpness of sight in the first place.

"Now look at this card." He was pointing at a familiar placard of letters. "What's the top line?"

The letters were so big and black that even their jiggling could not keep her from reading them correctly, and the pointer in the attendant's hand told her where to start. She could make out the next line and the next, and she saw the examiner and the starchy woman exchange puzzled glances: disappointed glances, as if they had hoped she needed glasses.

"Well," the man said, "you study it over some more, sister. And next time you come in, just keep saying to yourself, Nobody's going to take a crack at me even if I do make a mistake." He handed her another red and blue booklet with the same grinning cartoon on its cover. "Study this. And don't you be hard on her, sir. Some kids just naturally tie themselves into knots when they take tests."

"Consarn it," Pop sputtered. "Consarn the consarned book, anyway. Why can't they use plain American talk? But you just oncet get her in a car, mister, and you'll see she can drive slick as a whistle. Like enough she'll drive better than you can."

The official was already turning to another client. "Oh, she'll be okay," he said. "When she gets the hang of the questions and quits being scared of us, she'll do fine."

Glowering, Pop stamped out of the office. Florette's

oxfords spatted to a stop behind him to avoid the door he let swing in her face.

He started the truck before she was completely seated. She stole a glance at him. He was hunched forward, glaring ahead, his jaws working as if he were chewing. All the way home he said nothing, and Florette felt herself growing smaller and smaller.

"Get it, Florrie?" Mom asked, when Pop slammed into the house.

"Well, what happened?" Coral demanded from the sofa. "Run into somebody? Or park wrong? You're so cocky about your driving."

Pop hurled his cap on the TV and then shouted, as if infuriated because the limp cloth had not made the bang he wanted, "No, Florrie didn't get no license. Consarn the girl. I never thought I'd be pa to an idiot. And now looks like I'm pa to a pair of 'em."

Elvie began to whimper and scuttle toward his unfailing protector.

"You Elvie, shut your trap!" Pop yelled.

Elvie's whimper dwindled to a gasping sniffle. Whenever there was harshness in the home, he was like a flower touched by a frosty blast. Pop seldom directed the harshness toward him, except when he had had what Florette called a drop too much.

Even now, Pop cleared his throat and said, "You're okay, Elvie. It ain't no fault of yours. But this great girl—" His anger and his voice rose together. "This

102

great girl, going on seventeen and taller'n her Mom. Puts a man to shame, gawking over plain ever'day words as if she didn't know the American language —"

"Maybe Florrie couldn't help it," Mom interposed. "Like enough she was just too scared —"

"Couldn't help it! Too scared!" Pop mimicked, and kicked at his special rocker, so that the supporting brick gave up its responsibility. "If she wasn't a woman growed I'd scare her with a dose of my good old leather belt. Half a mind to anyway."

In homeroom next day Florette tried to busy herself so completely with books and papers that Miss Sansome would not ask about the test. She knew all the time that it wouldn't work. Ever since the affair of the stalled car, the teacher had been interested in her. Maybe it was better not to have them interested in her at all, the kind that looked at her as if she weren't there, or as if they wished she weren't.

She hurried her steps when she had to pass Miss Sansome on the way out. Her heart sucked sickeningly downward when the teacher's smooth cool hand touched her arm. She stopped, slipping out of the line.

"Did you take the examination yesterday, as you planned?"

Florette's reply was a mixture of nod and headshake.

"And you passed it all right?"

Florette stood silent, head hanging.

"Why, honey, what was wrong? Backing? Parking?

103

I'd hate to have to park myself, with an officer in the car."

Florette swallowed at the lump in her throat and squeezed her eyes shut against the threat of treacherous tears.

Miss Sansome patted her arm. "Listen, Florette. You wait until these boys and girls have cleared out, and we'll talk it over. But don't cry. This isn't the end of the world. You'll pass that old test yet."

Florette went and looked blindly at the window, seeing nothing beyond it. She wished the kids would take forever to clear out. On the other hand, Pop would be madder than a wet hen if she was late. He was still abed when she left the house that morning, and Mom had said reproachfully, as if it were all Florette's fault, that Pop was ailing worse than ever, or thought he was.

When Florette got home Pop would be sure to yell at her again. Miss Sansome wouldn't yell, but she might look at her the way the English teacher, Miss Orfut, did. Miss Sansome's hazel eyes could be cool, and her laughing lips could fold into a stern line.

At last all the pupils had left the room and Miss Sansome stopped moving around her desk. She called to Florette, still standing at the window and poking a finger unseeingly into a flowerpot.

"I would have sworn that a girl who knew cars as you do would pass that test like a breeze." Miss Sansome studied her over folded white hands. "But I suppose

104

anyone can get rattled. I remember to this day that I couldn't for the life of me think which way you cramp your wheels when you're parking downhill."

Unconsciously, Florette made an angular motion of her palms to indicate which way.

Miss Sansome laughed. "That's what I thought. You're a born driver and mechanic — and not just with one hand but with both of them. Ambidextrous, I've noticed. But I suppose even you could get rattled."

"I never came to that part of it," Florette blurted out, dismissing the cumbersome word, which she had heard applied to her before but had never understood. "They never gave me the chance to drive."

"But you surely studied the questions, Florette?"

"Yes'm." Florette pulled the red and blue booklet from her pocket. "Thank you for lending me your book."

Miss Sansome spoke briskly. "Well, let's see if we can get at the trouble. You read those questions and answers aloud slowly. Maybe then we can iron things out. Sit down, child, and take it easy."

Florette slipped into one of the front seats and turned to the first page. Her tongue went out and moistened her dry lips. "Where do you — do you want I should begin?"

Miss Sansome laughed reassuringly. "Begin at the beginning and read right on. We can take all the time we need."

Florette bent close above the open booklet. After

one dart of eyes at the teacher, she put a forefinger firmly on the page, moving it as she read. "One. Who — man-y dif-dif — " She gave up that word with a shake of her head — "Sha-ped Ro-ad sig — "

She knew it didn't make sense, but she plodded on to the end of the answer and then sat staring silently at the next one. The room was dreadfully hushed. Far away, outside, she could hear young voices shouting at each other. Indoors, feet scuffed through the corridors, and an electric polisher sang its high song along the tiled floor. At last she lifted her eyes to Miss Sansome's. It was the teacher's turn to moisten her lips, the teacher's turn to look as if she didn't understand something, and as if she didn't know what to say.

She cleared her throat. "Did they give you an eye examination yesterday, Florette?"

"Yes'm."

Miss Sansome's voice was hopeful. "Did they say you needed glasses?"

"No'm, they never."

"But still, those tests can't be at all accurate. Weren't your eyes examined back there where you lived before?"

"Yes'm. They always said my eyes were okay."

After a long moment Miss Sansome stirred. "Let's just try something," she said with a bright briskness that made Florette almost as uneasy as Pop's blustering. "You wait."

Smartly she clicked out of the room and back again,

carrying a small stack of books. One she laid open before Florette. "Read me a little of it." She said, laying a finger on the initial word.

Florette looked and relaxed. The print was big, and that always helped. After another glance at her teacher she followed the letters firmly with her finger. "The boy had a cat." Feeling silly, she read the text with only a few false starts, and Miss Sansome laid a second book on top of the first. Its print was almost as large, and Florette read, starting with the point Miss Sansome indicated, and pretending to herself that she was reading a picture book to Elvie. A third book followed, and a fourth, and Florette read slower and slower, because the letters were growing smaller and the words longer, and when they were crowded together they got mixed up with each other. When Miss Sansome slid out the first four books and laid the fifth before her, she stumbled hopelessly until the teacher interrupted her.

"That will do, Florette. It's a mystery to me what your teachers were doing — what they were thinking of, to let you go on to the seventh grade when you read at third-grade level."

Florette sat staring at her hands. She knew what those teachers had thought. They thought she was too dumb to know straight up. And after each one had kept her a couple of years, trying experiments with her with word cards and queer machines, they had passed her on to the next room and the next teacher. What else could they

107

do? Their classes were too big to keep her when she wasn't learning anything.

"Do you really try to read, Florette?" Miss Sansome's voice held the terrible patience that shriveled Florette inside.

"Yes'm. But I'm just — too dumb."

Miss Sansome shook her head in denial. "You surely should have had corrective reading. Your being ambidextrous — using both hands equally well — should have suggested something — I'll have a talk with Miss Orfut. And with the counselor. Of course you couldn't study the test questions when you couldn't read them. And without reading, you haven't developed a vocabulary, so even when your father read them to you — So how could you possibly get your license?"

Florette jerked erect and her wet eyes opened wide. "But I got to get that license. I got to."

"You don't have to if you can't."

"Yes'm, I got to. Pop's back is too bad. I got to take the truck out by myself when he can't. Else we — " She shrugged hopelessly. "The grocery store won't let us have no more grub without we pay for it. And the telephone company says we got to pay if we want to keep the phone. And the pump — " At the thought of it all, Florette's head bobbed down on her hands and heavy sobs shook her.

"There, there, honey, there, there," Miss Sansome said. "You're absolutely right. You can get that license.

A girl with so much spunk, and one who knows cars as you do. We're all dumb about something. It takes all kinds to make a world. As I've said before, I'd think I was made if I was as smart as you are about cars." Her hand was gently patting Florette, and hand and voice went on together, stroking Florette — and liking her. Florette grew still under that sound and touch.

At length the voice crisped again, with a pleasant do-something crispness. "Come along, child. Let's go to the teachers' lounge and wash your face and comb your hair. Nobody feels like anybody when her eyes and nose are red and swollen from crying. Then we'll slip down to the cafeteria and get a Coke and a sweet roll or dough-nut. I'm always as hungry as a bear by this time of day."

Mutely Florette followed her, and found the coolness of the water and the fragrance of the soap refreshing.

"Take my comb" — Miss Sansome had been holding it under the hot-water faucet — "if it's big enough to go through your lovely thick hair."

Florette did not try to say anything, until after Miss Sansome had got the Cokes from the cafeteria vending machine, and had asked one of the women who were operating the dishwashers to find them two fat, sugary doughnuts. When they had eaten and drunk, Florette managed a smile and a thank-you.

"And now," Miss Sansome said, dusting sugar from her immaculate sweater, "let's go at those driving ques-tions a different way. Let's kind of sneak up on them.

We can take a half hour yet this afternoon, and go on from there tomorrow."

Florette was shaking a hopeless head. "It isn't a speck of use. I'm just plain dumb."

"You hush!" Miss Sansome took her hand as if they were little girls, and ran lightly with her, up the stairs and into the homeroom. "Now look, Florette: that first — no, second — question, about the shapes and the meanings of the road signs. You watch." With swift strokes of the chalk, she drew on the blackboard a square, a triangle, three more shapes. "How many, Florette?"

"Well, of course, five."

"Remember that: five." Her eraser scuffed rapidly across the figures. "Now come and make them for me. Please add and name them."

Florette did.

"Fine," said the teacher, with an I-told-you-so expression. "Now we'll see what they mean."

"I know, when I see them alongside the road," Florette murmured.

11

Florette got home late that day, and had to meet three pairs of eyes and a pelting of questions. Elvie was the only one who did not cross-examine her. He flew uncritically into her arms.

"Five o'clock straight up," Pop grunted. "That's fine. Just dandy. Not even can't she drive the truck for her sick father: she can't even show up in time to go along and help him h'ist."

"Now you're here," Mom put in, "how about peeling some spuds and getting supper started? I been having one of my all-gone spells."

"Okay," Florette agreed, cuddling Elvie, "though seems funny Coral can't never — I did think to mend this dress neater and wash it good. Some way our clo'es don't look so clear, Mom."

But she did put Elvie down and go at peeling the potatoes, shutting her thoughts against Pop's fuming. Even though she still had little hope of passing the test, her world did not seem quite so dreary as it had. Maybe it was what Miss Sansome said about its taking all kinds. Or maybe it was the way she said it, as if she really liked Florette. You could stand an awful lot if someone liked you. It made you feel like somebody. That Fred Barlow, too —

After she had washed the dishes, she changed her dress, ripped out the big stitches, sewed it again, sewed on a button that was nearer matching. Even then she had a little time to fool with the old Oliver typewriter and look through the tattered book that had accompanied it. She did not understand the purpose of the book, but it had some pretty sayings in it. Some of them that she struggled with made no sense at all, because the words were too long and too strange. But she came across two that she liked so well that she copied them on the battered machine, which had a fairly good ribbon. She copied them because the English class was supposed to bring to school next day something they had read and liked.

In a book from the dump she had found creamy fly-leaves that were nicer paper than her ruled tablet afforded. She trimmed off the yellowed edges and used one for her mottoes, spoiling the first but succeeding pretty well with the second, and even making a border for it, with the little star she found on the keyboard. Carefully then, with much consulting of the book, she penciled in the letters that the typewriter would not print.

The task took the whole evening, and she was glad the dress was the drip-dry kind, so that she did not have to iron it that night. She did wash her slip, and take an extra bath, with scanty water because Pop kept warning them not to waste it, with the well so near dry. You didn't realize how clean-clean-clean some people were until you got close to them, as she had to Miss Sansome that day. It was a smooth, sweet cleanness, a fresh, crisp cleanness —

She looked around the house, and her small happiness slipped. "Mom," she said, "if you felt okay tomorrow, couldn't you mop up the floor with real hot suds?"

Mom yawned. "Listen at her. Like your pop says, you dawdle around after school and then you stick up your nose at your mom's housekeeping. If I was young and strong like you, Florette, I'd sure keep the place spic and span — if anybody could keep such a lousy house spic and span. Which I doubt." Now she was glaring at Pop.

"But, Mom, when the Man comes to see Elvie — "

Pop's bitter guffaw interrupted her. "Yes, listen at the girl. When he comes, she says. Don't fool yourself: he ain't a-going to come. If we was rich folks, sure. If we lived in a swell house and wore swell clo'es, sure. But where do us poor folks get it? In the neck, ever' time."

"Oh, Pop!"

"Don't Oh-Pop me. It's the truth I'm telling you. If we'd drove up to that office in a shiny new car today, and you had went in, all la-de-da in silk and fur, you think they wouldn't have fixed it so you'd get the license? Sure they would. Don't fool yourself. And this here high muckamuck, he won't put himself out for the likes of us. You put that in your pipe and smoke it."

"I sure hope he doesn't," said Coral, intensely concentrated in putting up her hair on rollers.

"You can say that again," agreed Mom pulling Elvie out of Florette's arms and squeezing him till he cried wrathfully. "Sister may want you should get took away from us, but not your mom, honey-baby."

Next morning Florette shyly showed her mottoes to Miss Sansome before taking them to English class. "Wasn't it kind of funny," she said, "that you told me this one yesterday and I found it in the tough typing book last night?"

"You mean touch typing — or was it a joke? And the other one is just as true," Miss Sansome hurried on, perhaps guessing that it had not been a joke. "Will you read them aloud, Florette?"

Florette bent her head over the page. " 'It takes all kinds to make a world.' 'It is not what we have that —' " She hesitated, and Miss Sansome prompted, " 'That counts.' " — " 'that counts, but what we do with it.' "

"You read that very well," Miss Sansome complimented her.

"I learned them off by heart," Florette admitted, "all but that one word." As she went on toward class, she moved her lips, silently repeating the sentences. She liked them. And they must be true, since they were printed in a book.

Again that afternoon Miss Sansome gave her the hour of coaching. " 'What qualifications are essential to being a safe driver?' Listen hard, Florette, and look at the book, too."

"They're awful big words," Florette murmured, pushing the hair away from her hot face.

"That's true," Miss Sansome agreed. "It just means what do you have to be like, to be a safe driver? And the answer is, you must have knowledge, that is knowing, and ability, being able. Now I'll read the question the way it's written, and you watch the big words and answer me. I wish I were better at this, Florette."

"Yes'm," Florette said, when Miss Sansome had read again. "You got to know all about everything, and you got to be able to drive good."

"What knowledge is required? That is: What do you have to know? And the answer is that you have to know the traffic laws and the driving rules, and how people are likely to act, driving or walking."

They went over twenty of the questions, and then Miss Sansome repeated them all, her eyes anxious and one finger tapping the desk. Sometimes Florette's answers came slowly, but they came.

"Your memory is unusually good," the teacher praised, looking at her watch and at the schoolroom clock, closing the book and pushing back from her desk, all at once. But she did pause to say, "With that memory, if you listen hard in classes like English and Socks, you ought to get a lot, even though your reading is a handicap. I've got to fly, honey. Till tomorrow! Twenty more questions!"

"And there's two hundred!" Florette felt panicky.

"We'll beat them yet," Miss Sansome assured her. "Even if we have to take the lunch hour for it, too."

A few of the younger children were swinging and sliding on the school grounds as Florette started home, and a big boy stood accurately firing pebbles at a street sign. As she came abreast of him, he turned and exclaimed, "Well, look who's here! If it isn't Florette, the girl wizard! What you been up to, getting kept in so long?"

It was Fred Barlow, and Florette felt herself blushing. "You throw real straight," she said. "I'm pretty good, too." She plopped down her books, picked up a pebble and hit the sign with a thud. Then, obeying an impulse she did not fully understand, she threw another, and let it fall short of the mark. "Not so good as you," she said, shaking her head.

"Mighty sharp for a girl. But how come you were kept in?"

"Miss Sansome's coaching me for a test. For a driver's license. I flunked it," she said with a rush.

"Sure enough? So did I. All those dumb questions about how many lights on a truck and how many feet you keep behind, and all that junk. Made me so mad I haven't tried again. Your cousin pass it?"

"My cousin? Oh, Coral. No, she isn't old enough for anything but a learner's license. And anyway she's going to wait till Pop gets a decent car."

"She's sure pretty," Fred said.

116

"Sure is," Florette agreed, though agreeing hurt.

"Bet she couldn't throw like you, not to save her neck. To say nothing of fixing a balky car. And she looks awful sissy. Her eyes aren't as pretty as yours, Florette."

Not only Florette's eyes but her mouth flew open in astonishment. "Who you kidding?"

He shook his head. "Yours are different. Nobody ever tell you? That real light brown and the curly lashes — I can't figure out what it is about them —"

"I like blue better. You make me think of a boy back home, but his were brown. He was a real nice boy. Georgie Gaynor."

"Your boyfriend?" he asked quickly.

She shook her head. "It was my sis — my cousin he liked."

"More fool he," Fred said matter-of-factly, falling into step beside her.

She darted a quick glance around to see if anyone was watching. Strange to have a boy walking her home.

"Gosh," he said, reaching over to take her books, "I never noticed how many you were lugging."

Automatically Florette held on, and presently they were both pulling at them. Then he gave a heave and got them away from her, almost falling with the force of the pull. He burst out laughing. "Anybody'd think we were having a fight."

After a moment Florette laughed, too.

His sweater was clean and new, and his shirt collar over it as clean as white paper. Florette was thankful

117

that she had washed and ironed and mended her dress.

He said, "You must be a swell basketball player."

"Might be okay, if I could ever get to ninth grade."

He said, "You been sick, they say, and it kept you back."

"Yes, I was in the hospital five years." But she could not leave it that way. She blurted out, "That's an awful whopper. I'm just — slow, that's all there is to it."

He stared at her, brow puckered. He won't have anything more to do with such a dumbbell, she thought.

But then he said, "Gosh, isn't it funny how things are? None of those kids that can read like professors can make out what's wrong with a car. They read books and you read machines. Folks are sure different."

" 'It takes all kinds to make a world,' " Florette quoted, looking sidewise to see if he liked it.

"Yeah, I've heard my folks say that. And isn't it the truth?"

"This where you turn off?" she inquired, when they came to a crossroad. Then she blushed, for he would know that she had watched where he went.

"But a little extra walk is good for me," he said. "Two pounds overweight. Gee, there's a real early sand lily."

"Sand lily?" she said absently. "Fred, Pop and Mom are both kind of under the weather, so maybe you better not come any farther."

She knew it sounded silly, but suddenly she felt as maybe Coral did when Jane saw their home in all its rusty shabbiness. And dirt. A sight of it might make

Fred feel as if she was nothing but trash.

"Well," he said indignantly, "how's that for a brush-off?"

She did not reach for her books. Peering toward that shabby house, her eyes had narrowed. "Look," she cried, "isn't that smoke?"

"Sure it's smoke. Why not? There's almost always smoke from that old dump. Folks around here been asking the city to close it —"

Without more words, she began to run down the road. She heard Fred's feet pounding behind her. He would have to see their house, then. But it wouldn't make any difference in the long run, because he'd soon find out she wasn't his kind —

As she drew nearer she could see the flames creeping over from the dump, burning a strip of prairie halfway to their house. Still no one came out. She quickened her pace and so did the boy behind her.

She was breathless by the time she pelted through the yard and yanked open the door, Fred following close. Pop's truck was parked in the yard, but Pop was no-where about. Likely at the tavern. Coral was not there either, and Mom and Elvie were asleep on the sofa.

Without pausing to waken them, Florette leaped across the room and jerked the telephone from its cradle. No dial tone. Her heart felt as if steel fingers squeezed it. Frantically, uselessly, she dialed the operator's num-ber.

"Can't you get the fire department?" Fred gasped.

119

She shook her head. "Phone's dead."

"Oh, no!"

She needn't tell him of the repeated warnings as to nonpayment of their bill. "I better get water and douse things round the house —" She dashed to the kitchen for the buckets, then out to the pump.

Flinging herself on the handle bodily, she rode it down. Only a scanty trickle came out. "Pop says it's most dry —"

"Oh, no!" Fred croaked again. "Better run to a neighbor —"

But Florette was already scrambling into the truck. Before she could get it started Fred was in the seat beside her. "I'll go to the nearest filling station to phone," she explained. "Surer that way. Don't know what neighbors have phones."

The truck went rattling and banging over the rough road, picking up speed as she gave it the gas. Then it went at its fastest clip along the pavement toward the nearest station. Fast and faster —

"G-gosh," stammered Fred, "there's a cop — "

Florette bounded in her seat as the shrill demand of a siren pierced her ears. But she did not slacken until the official car had zoomed to overtake her and wave her to the curb.

"Listen, mister," she said, "look back yonder. The dump's set fire to the weeds, and it's awful close to our house —"

120

The officer sniffed the air, but the wind was in the other direction. "Sure enough?" he asked Fred.

"Yes, sir."

"Go on, then, and I'll follow. Filling station next block. Say, why didn't you phone from home?"

"Phone dead." Fred tossed back the answer as they sped on.

When they reached the station, Florette leaped out and ran for the telephone, visible just inside. "How do I get the fire engine?" she called to the officer, and he followed and told her the number slipping a dime into the slot when she started to dial without doing so.

In only another minute she was climbing into the truck, Fred with her. "Our house," she called to the officer. "I got to get there —"

"I'll follow," he replied, with a mingling of grimness and curiosity.

The sight was beautiful but fearful. The flames, pale in the sunlight, raced on a front a half block wide toward the Cochrane house. People were running now from other houses, but Florette could not yet see Mom and Elvie. Nor Pop. Evidently the fire had not been noticed at the tavern.

Some of the neighbors were slapping at the flames with what looked like wet gunnysacks. Others playing hoses on their roofs. The Cochrane house stood undefended. Before Florette had time to despair, the high warnings of the fire department tore through the air. A big red engine was racing noisily toward them, firemen piling out and attaching their hoses to the nearest hydrant, a half block away.

Florette dashed into the house to see that Mom and Elvie were all right. She came out, lugging the child, his sleepy eyes widening at the fire and the commotion, his hands grabbing at Florette's hair and dress as he saw the strangers. Mom watched from the doorway, elbows in palms. No one said anything much until the flames were conquered, the ground thoroughly drenched, and the firemen preparing to depart.

Then the police officer beckoned from his car. This is it, Florette thought, silently approaching him, while Elvie hid his face in her neck.

"Let's see your driver's license, miss."

"I — I haven't got none."

He whistled. "Don't you know you've broken the law, driving without a license?"

"She had to get to a telephone," Fred put in, stationing himself beside her. "Like I told you, theirs went dead. She tried everything she could. No water, either —"

"We only got a well," Florette offered. "Looked like I had to —"

"The destruction of the poor is their poverty." The words sounded funny, as if he were a preacher saying a text. "But you better get that license pronto. I won't charge you this time, not under the circumstances. But if I catch you driving without a license again — or speeding like you did — " His scowl broke up in a smile. He reached out and patted her shoulder, before he put his car in gear and purred away. "But the law is the law, young lady," he called back to her. "And it's for your own protection."

Fred was poking a finger at Elvie, and Elvie was coming far enough out of his sister's shoulder to roll one eye at him. "Your little brother?" Fred asked.

Florette swung Elvie round for a better view, though he scrabbled ineffectually to get back into hiding. "My brother Elvie," she said, "with jam all over his face."

"He sure likes you," Fred observed as the child settled determinedly into Florette's neck.

"And I sure like him," Florette replied, smoothing his hair with her free hand. "It's what they call cerebral palsy," she said defensively. "He's smart inside, only he can't get it out."

Slowly they walked around toward the door, Florette laughing shyly as they passed the part of the house she had painted. "Soon as I get that license, so me and Pop can take in more loads, I'm going to paint the whole place. Two coats."

Fred looked from her to Elvie and then at the length of painted boards. "Know something?" he said abruptly, "You're a kind of a swell kid."

"Oh my no." Florette hid her face in Elvie's mist of curls.

"Look," he said, "if you're aiming to bone up for that old driver's test — well, so'm I. Look," he repeated, "how's if I walk you home the nights old Sansome coaches you? Then we could kind of practice on each other."

Florette drew a breath so deep that it hurt. He had seen the house and Mom and Elvie, and yet— She hoped Pop wouldn't come just at that moment from the tavern. That might be too much, all at once. She could picture him, stepping with exaggerated care, and owlishly staring at them. He might sweep off his cap and give them formal greetings if he were at one stage, or glare and snarl at them if he were at another.

Thank goodness, Pop wasn't anywhere in sight.

"Why, sure," Florette told Fred, looking down into Elvie's face. "I don't mind. If you really want to."

12

FLORETTE both longed and dreaded going to school next morning. Fred might have thought it over, and remembered the house, and Mom's dingy dress and everything, and realized that she wasn't, after all, the kind of girl he wanted to walk home. She didn't blame him. She could imagine some of the other boys hooting at him, "Say, I wouldn't be caught dead with a girl that looked like that. Dumb, too."

And the first person she saw on the school grounds was Fred. He wasn't looking at her. He was talking excitedly to a bunch of kids who crowded round him with wide eyes, open mouths, exclamations. Florette was about to sneak past them into the refuge of the schoolhouse, but she had no chance.

"There she is," Fred shouted. "There's the gal wonder. Ought to see her handle that truck. Sure made it say uncle. Broke the speed laws and then set her down neat as a whistle. Hi, Florette, don't forget we got us a date."

Florette smiled, finding no words ready.

"What do you know?" he went on addressing the throng of classmates. "We both flunked the question and answer part of the driver's test, Florette and me. Didn't get our licenses. So we're kind of going to help each other practice. Rest of you guys can keep off. I saw her first."

They all stared at her, and she was glad she had primped a little, even with Pop making fun of her for doing it.

Jane Brown was at the edge of the group, and said, "Fred, you're a pig. I need help, too, I'll tell the world. I thought maybe Florette would show me something about parking. If I could sort of rehearse you on your questions at noon, Flo, would you maybe give me some pointers?"

Though some of the kids regarded her dubiously, the only evidently disapproving one was Coral. Yet after school that day she did approach Florette in her homeroom. "How long you likely to be here this time?" she inquired. "Pop will be fit to be tied."

"You can just tell Pop — or your Uncle Jim — that the more time I study these questions the quicker I get to drive the truck," Florette said coldly.

She was thinking that her status at school had risen enough so that Coral would have been willing to walk home with her and Fred. Florette didn't want her to. Fred might think he didn't like Coral, but boys were boys, and Florette dreaded competition with her sister's picture-book prettiness.

Miss Sansome said, "Well, Florette, you're quite the heroine today. Everyone's saying you drove like a demon and saved the whole town from fiery destruction."

"That's a great big story," Florette said. But she smiled uncontrollably at her homeroom teacher, and set about the afternoon's drilling with new confidence. Though the reading was no easier, she seemed to remember everything more clearly. Maybe it was because she was so happy.

"We've covered a lot of ground," Miss Sansome said when their time was used. "Keep it up at this clip, Florette, and you'll be ready before you know it."

Still smiling, Florette gathered up her books and went out to her locker to get her sweater. But maybe Fred wouldn't have waited all this time —

He had, sitting on the parallel bars with his legs wrapped around them while he scowled over that familiar red and blue booklet. She was passing the bars before he saw her.

He leaped off and grabbed her books. "Hi! Began to be scared you'd gone off and left me. Listen: how many road signs and what shape and what do they mean?"

"Five: triangle, rectangle — " Florette rattled off the list and gave the meanings. "Now it's your turn."

They walked on through the May sunshine, and the trees had never been so lovely as now, in their fresh, lacy green. Birds were singing the same song over and over, faster and faster, as if their joy were too much to be endured.

"What should a driver do in going down a steep hill?" Florette asked, and broke off to say, "Those little cutie birds. Looks like they got red on their necks and heads."

"Yeah, house finches," said Fred. "You shift transmission to a lower gear —"

The yard where the dogs lived was full of apple trees, big white and pink bouquets. Florette stood still to draw deep breaths of their fragrance while the dogs, leaping and snarling toward them, stopped their outcry and sniffed at her skirts, wagging their tails and their whole bodies.

"Guess they know you," said Fred. "Say, do you like lilacs?"

She nodded. "I just love 'em. We had a bush in Nebraska."

"Ours are in bloom — early spring this year — and you can smell them a block away," Fred boasted. "If you'll walk around by our house I'll pick you a bunch."

"Wouldn't your mom mind?"

"Mother's a good joe. She'd be tickled to have you have some. Well, how's about it?" he persisted, as they came to the crossroad.

"It's too late anyway to help Pop," Florette considered. "If he was fixing to haul he's already gone." She stole a glance downward at dress and shoes, and pulled off her faded sweater. Carried over her arm it didn't look too bad. She jerked her head in embarrassed assent. "I'd sure like to have the lilacs, if your mom —"

Her heart was pumping hard when they came to a block of small houses and Fred said, "That one's ours, third from the corner." Would it be so far better than the dump house that she would be shamed by it?

Inside the third yard, behind a white picket fence, raced a bulky dog with long white hair over his eyes. He was not barking, but whining with evident delight.

"Hi, Raggsy," Fred greeted him, reaching over and unhooking the gate. "He won't bite, Florette."

"Wouldn't Elvie love him!" Florette murmured as the sheep dog pounced on Fred, forepaws on his shoulders and lavish tongue on his face.

"I'll walk him over there some day," said Fred. "Raggsy, quit your slobbering."

"That you, Freddie?" called a brisk voice.

Florette drew a deep breath and hesitated on the porch as Fred pushed open the screen door and went in. It was a shiny porch, even its floorboards glossy. The house wasn't much bigger than the Cochranes', and that was a comfort.

"Here's Florette Cochrane, the girl where the fire was," Fred was shouting.

"Well, my land," his mother scolded, "is that any kind of manners, Freddie? Hollering as if I was a mile away. And letting the door bang shut and your company stuck on the porch? Come right in, Florette, and don't mind my clumsy boy. Acts like he was born in a barn."

Florette's feet got in her way as she went in, but one look at Fred's mother relieved some of her fears. Mrs. Barlow was just a nice, plain woman in a nice clean house dress, with her hair frizzed more than Miss Sansome would like it. Her face was pleasant, but not too smily to be real. She looked hard at Florette, and why wouldn't she? A mom must want to know what kind of girl her son was walking home.

"Well, why not?" Mrs. Barlow agreed. "Only I'll do the cutting. He leaves the bushes looking like picked hens, Florette."

"What's to eat?" Fred demanded. "Smells like cookies."

Mrs. Barlow led the way into the kitchen and took a pair of shears from a drawer, nodding toward the table, where sugary rounds were spread to cool. "Put some on a plate for Florette and you. And what about milk to go with them? I'll be getting the flowers."

Fred got the milk from the refrigerator and poured two tall glasses of it. "Help yourself to cookies," he said, hurrying to take a deep, cold swallow.

Florette took a cooky, noticing the circular opening that showed the filling of raisins or jam. "It looks good," she said.

Fred's mouth was crowded with the bite he took. "Mother isn't bad at cookies and stuff," he said thickly.

These were so sweet and warm and spicy that Florette was tempted to stuff half of hers into her mouth at one bite as Fred had done. Remembering how Miss Sansome had eaten the doughnut, she restrained herself and savored it slowly. Mom used to bake cookies and pies and cake, before Elvie was born. Florette had almost forgotten those long-ago baking days.

This was a shiny kitchen, with shiny linoleum floor and counters and glossy paint on all the woodwork. When Florette had been driving for Pop awhile, they could maybe afford linoleum. But before that, if they scrubbed the floor with lye — and if she starched the curtains —

Mrs. Barlow had the lilacs ready by the time Florette and Fred had eaten two cookies apiece and drunk their milk. Florette buried her face in the fresh, cool sweetness of the bouquet. "They got a smell like nothing else in this world," she said.

"The tulips don't smell so nice, but I always think they're one of the cheeriest flowers," said Mrs. Barlow. "The early ones are through blooming but the parrots will soon be out, and you must have some — you so partial to flowers."

As they walked toward the dump, Fred carried Florette's books while she carried the lilacs.

"Your mom's awfully nice," she said.

"I told her and Dad how you handled the truck the day of the fire, Florette. Golly, I wouldn't have believed that truck could go so fast."

Florette laughed suddenly. "The fire scared me stiff, but I sure did get a big kick out of driving like that. And I really had to," she added defensively.

For a moment she lived those minutes over again. She, Florette Cochrane, flying along with all that power in her hands. The experience had been brand-new and glorious. An edge of her mind wondered whether

Pop could possibly feel like that when he had taken a few drinks. As if everything that had been cluttering up the world was out from under foot — as if he was as good as anyone —

But as they came in sight of the house her step slackened. "Maybe this time you better not come all the way, Fred. Pop, he's liable to be real put out with me for not getting home sooner."

"When you only stayed to work on those old questions?"

"Pop doesn't go to be mean. But when his back hurts him so bad he can't work, and he don't get ahead at all — well, he sort of takes it out on us."

At Fred's expression, Florette hurried on, feeling a sudden need to stand up for her father. "You see, Fred —" Her pace was so slow now that she was almost standing still — "Pop was a good farmer, but the big farms, and the big machines, well, they just squeezed the life out of our little place. You know what? At the farm closest to us, one of the machines — just one, mind you — cost more than Pop got for our whole farm."

She tried again. "A farmer's kind of proud, I guess. And when Pop doesn't have anything to be proud of — well, seems like you've got to have something to be proud of, or you're sunk."

With a new clearness she was thinking that just a little speck of pride had done something for her. And poor Pop —

"You sure do think things out," said Fred, handing

over the books. "Okay, if that's the way you want it."

She smiled at him. "I had a real nice time. Please thank your mom again for me."

"Till tomorrow."

Till tomorrow — till tomorrow — till tomorrow. The words kept time to her feet, or her feet kept time to the words, with a little extra skip every so often.

Pop was home, and though he was lying on the couch, he said, "How come you walked a different way? And who was that young whippersnapper? You worked it to keep away from home that much longer?"

"Me and Fred Barlow, we're going over the driving questions. He flunked the test, too." Florette was trying to remember her new thoughts about Pop, but the old resentment flared up in her.

"Hmph. Never supposed they was anyone else dumb enough. And did that mean you had to walk way round Robin Hood's barn?"

Florette dropped down on the floor to look at a huddle of vases that Pop had brought in from a load. One of them had soft colors that ran into each other so you couldn't tell where rose stopped and gray or green began. Florette held against it the plumes of lilac, pink-lavender and deep purple and white. She sucked in her breath. It looked nice.

"Where'd you get them flowers?"

"We went past his house and his mom gave them to me. And cookies and milk," Florette added rapidly, pouring water into the vase, and finding that it oozed out through cracks in the base. Fortunately, or it wouldn't have been thrown away. She set a glass jar inside it and put the water and the flowers into that.

"Listen to me." Pop was leaning up on one elbow and shaking a forefinger at her. "My kids don't go around mooching handouts."

Florette set the bouquet on the radio and arranged the flowers and her thoughts. Sure, Pop was proud, but why did he have to take it out on her?

"I never asked for a thing. They were just being folksy. Maybe I could sort of pay it back by making some san'wiches and Kool-Aid. If Fred wants to practice those questions again."

Pop subsided, rumbling. "I don't know's I want any young punks hanging round my girls. Things you hear nowadays —"

"More I practice, sooner I get my license." Florette's voice barely quavered as she thus defied him.

"Florette's making a dead set at that Fred Barlow." Coral was hunched before the TV, doing something to her nails. It was beyond Florette, how much time her sister could spend on ten fingernails. Red polish, pink polish, even a kind of pearl colored polish —

"And that's a black lie," Florette snapped. She did not add, as she was tempted to, What about you, missy, and that Sid Gapson, the one who lights a cigarette the minute he's out of sight of the schoolhouse?

She put the question to her sister, shaping with her lips the name Sid Gapson, and accenting it with her stare. Silently, because she was in the habit of hiding Coral's slight scrapes from Pop. Sometime she'd just let them all out, and see what would happen to Miss Coral then.

"Well, if you've done with your gabbling and your messing round with the posies, how about rustling up some grub? Your mom don't seem to feel up to nothing but watching the pitchers."

Mom said, "What you been doing yourself, Jim Cochrane? And I'd thank you to leave this baby sleep a little longer, if you got no objection." Mom, too, was stationed before the TV, hands clasped round the sleeping Elvie.

Florette rummaged on the shelves for the makings of supper, at the same time thinking of the proposed after-school snack. Most boys liked peanut butter and jelly sandwiches — if there was enough peanut butter left, and enough jelly.

But what would Mrs. Barlow be saying to Fred about her? It looked like he and his folks were real close, and talked about things. Would she be saying, What kind of girl is that, you picked to walk home? Talk about being born in a barn! You'd a sight better stick to that nice little Kitty Perry.

Florette had seen him walking off with Kitty, with her pineapple haircut and her soft, smooth sweaters and her flirty switching skirts.

The next day seemed especially long. At noon Jane had brought her tray of lunch and plumped down beside

Florette, who was eating from her paper sack. "If we eat fast," Jane coaxed, "maybe you could go out and show me just how you park so neat. Everyone says you're a whiz at it."

After the parking lesson Jane had had time to review her on the first fifty questions.

But at last school was out, and Florette's hour of coaching with Miss Sansome was over. She dawdled for a minute at her locker, because even yet she was afraid that when she went to the door Fred would not be waiting for her. She walked slowly to the entry, and her mouth was dry when she looked toward the parallel bars.

13

Aɴᴅ Fred was there.

The reviewing went on rapidly as they sauntered homeward. At the crossroads he paused and questioned her with his eyes.

"You sick and tired of peanut butter and jelly san'-wiches?" she asked, surprised at the ease of her first invitation.

"Gosh, no, who is? But you needn't put yourself out."

Florette flashed him a smile. That was easy, too. She felt like smiling. She felt like laughing out loud. "Race you home!" she cried, and started out at a long lope.

She had hoped the truck would be gone, but it was still there. "There's a nice soft chair for you," she said, pointing at a rock in the middle of the yard, and feeling gay and witty. "I'll be with you soon as I fix the Kool-Aid." She took her books from him and ran into the house.

She meant to bring Elvie out. He would have been disappointed if she had failed him. But he and Mom were asleep, as they so often were.

But Pop was awake. "You fetch home that scala-

wag?" he growled from the sofa. "Where at's your sister?"

"Coral will be along," Florette answered, hoping that
she would. "Pop, wouldn't a peanut butter and jelly
san'wich taste good to you? And some Kool-Aid?" She
had already located the sandwiches so carefully made
and wrapped that morning. Luckily no one had found
them.

Pop grumbled, "Bah! Junk! Turns my stomach to
think of it."

Lightheartedly Florette ran out with a full plate, and
a second time with the two best jelly glasses, filled with
pink beverage. "It isn't nice and cold like the milk yesterday," she apologized. "No refrigerator yet. When
I can take the route for Pop we'll soon get caught up so
we can buy some of those things. Now it seems like
every dollar that comes in has to go out just as fast.
Guess we aren't used to having to run to the store for
anything we want to eat. On the farm you got your own
vegetables and fruit and eggs and all."

Here was another surprise: the way the words poured
out. Elvie had been the only one she could talk to like
that, full pelt.

"Gosh." Fred took a large bite of sandwich and
washed it down with a larger gulp of Kool-Aid. "You
can't tell me anything I don't know about the dollars
getting away from you. My dad lost his job in the print-
shop. New machines that took the place of a whole

138

gang of men. Cheaper. Dad pounded the pavements here and in Denver and couldn't find a thing. Finally he set up a little radio repair shop. This town was short of radio repairmen, good ones. But there awhile it was nip and tuck for the Barlows. Dad put in a garden and raised chickens and rabbits. And Mom canned and froze what we couldn't eat fresh. Gosh, no, you can't tell me anything about those disappearing dollars." He was eying the remaining sandwiches. "Guess I've had my share. You made them just right, Flor. Mind if I call you Flor?"

Shaking her head, Florette held out the plate. "I don't hardly ever take more than one. You finish up." Today hers had tasted so good that she could have eaten five.

"It isn't that Florette isn't an all-right name," Fred apologized after another swallow. "Only it doesn't seem to fit you exactly."

"Just about the way a little pink hairbow would," she agreed. "Mom never did have much that was pretty. I guess that's why she called us Florette and Coral and Elvis. I often wish I could change my name. I'd give anything to be Eleanor, or Mary, or Jane. But it always seemed like it would be mean to Mom."

"You're pretty nice to your folks, aren't you?"

She was glad she need not answer yes or no. There'd been so many times when she hadn't felt a bit nice.

"You reckon we could take the test in another week?" she asked shyly.

In another week they seemed to be ready. "I do believe you know the book by heart," Miss Sansome said to Florette. She looked past her at someone standing in the door. "This girl has what I'd call a phenomenal memory," she said.

Glancing round, Florette encountered the skeptical eyes of Miss Orfut, her English teacher. She's saying, Well, it's new to me that there's anything phe-phe — good about her.

"You know," Miss Sansome went on, as Miss Orfut withdrew, shaking her head, "we're through early today. Why don't I take you down to have your examination right now? Surprise your father and mother?"

Was Miss Sansome thinking that if Florette failed again she would not have to report it at home? "You reckon I can't make it?"

"Goodness, I know you will. I want to be there to give three cheers."

Florette let out her held breath. After all, she did know all those answers, didn't she? "I reckon Fred's out there, waiting like usually," she suggested.

"I always did like Fred," Miss Sansome approved. "We could take him along, if you think he's ready for the test."

"Yes'm, if we go over that 137 all the way down. Likely they'd never ask it. But I tell him over and over that it's at least five hundred feet, and he still says three hundred."

When they told Fred of their project, he agreed

heartily. "Why, sure thing. We're as good as we'll ever be. But you know we've got to take the driving test in the vehicle we'll be using. Your pop's truck, Flor, and my dad's Chevvy."

Miss Sansome made a laughing face of disgust. "Entirely slipped my mind. Where does that leave us? Will your pop be out hauling, Florette?"

"Not likely. His back was extra bad this morning."

"Well, then," Miss Sansome cried. "What are we waiting for?"

She drove them down to the Cochrane house and went in with Florette. Pop was sunk deep in his old chair, looking drawn and bloodless. He sat erect, catching back a groan, and gave a triple nod at the teacher.

"Mr. Cochrane," she asked with a pixyish smile like a small girl who's up to mischief, "could we borrow your truck for a surprise errand? It happens I can't take my car. We'll promise to bring it back in as good shape as we took it. And we'll leave mine here for security."

Pop gave a startled glance out of the window at the trim white compact. "But you wouldn't want to ride in that old rattletrap, Mrs. Sansome?"

"That's just what I want. And in a couple of hours we'll tell you the whole story."

Brow puckered, he raised himself enough to pull the keys out of his pocket, shaking his head dubiously.

"Thank you, Pop," Florette said breathlessly as she took them. "Bye, Mom. Bye, Elvie-angel. You mean you're willing to ride in this thing?" she asked Miss Sansome as they ran out to the dingy truck with its flaming red patch and its rather odorous interior.

"Well, what do you think I am? A wax doll? And this way it's legal for you to drive it."

All three climbed into the cab and were off, Pop and Mom, with Elvie, standing on the porch to see them go. On the way they stopped at Mr. Barlow's shop, and he came striding out to greet the teacher and meet Florette. He looked a little like Fred, grown thicker in the middle, and with his hair retreating so far that he was forehead up to his crown. He was in rolled-up shirt-sleeves, and held his greasy fingers spread apart, saying, "Right in the middle of a dirty overhaul job, ladies. Something I can do for you and this good-for-nothing boy of mine?"

When they explained the need of his car, he said, "Well, sure. That's no million-dollar touch. Guess I'll have time to clean up before you need it. I'll just park it out in front and walk back, Fred. You can bring it when you're through. Or if you flunk it again, you little bum, you can phone me."

When they had driven up and parked as near as possible to the traffic office where she had met her shattering defeat, Florette caught sight of a familiar figure emerging from the door. It was the patrolman whom she had met the day of the fire. He recognized her at once.

"Well, if it isn't my young lawbreaker! Did you know

142

she was a criminal?" he laughingly asked Miss Sansome. "I wondered whether you'd been in to get things fixed up, young lady."

"This very hour," said Miss Sansome.

"But, mister," Florette said, "I've kept watching for you, to pay back that money. And now I haven't any on me."

"What money's that?"

"The dime. For the telephone."

Though he laughed, shaking his head and saying, "What's a dime between friends?" Fred produced the coin and handed it to him.

"I'll pay him back," Florette earnestly told the patrolman.

"If you ever see the guy again," he twitted her.

Somehow the encounter had made everything easier and more casual when the three of them were ushered into the end of the big room.

"You're giving oral tests nowadays, aren't you?" Miss Sansome said. "I'm glad. For one thing, it's quicker."

"Yes, we can get through this in short order," the attendant said. "They've both seen the questions before," he added as if recognizing them. "Here's a room for each of them. If you'll just wait outside, ma'am."

"Now," said another uniformed man, when he and Florette were established in one of the small rooms, "why don't we start with the road signs? Look through this glass and tell me what they mean."

143

It was a lucky omen, that this should be the first question. Her fortune continued good. She knew most of the rest of the answers as well as she did that often practiced one. She had a phenom-something memory, and that meant it was better than most, instead of worse. With few hesitations and fewer errors, she sailed through the whole list that the attendant asked, and emerged a minute ahead of Fred.

Their examiners came out soon afterward. "Congratulations," said one. "Ninety-six and ninety. Passing and then some."

Florette closed her eyes and exhaled a long breath of relief. "Oh! Ninety! I'm sure thankful to get ninety."

"Ninety-six," her examiner corrected. "The young man has the ninety. But that's plenty good for one of us males. Points to spare."

Florette felt herself smiling foolishly.

"What you know, Flor?" Fred grumbled. "One of those I missed was 137. I said three hundred feet."

"Now someone will take each of you out for your driving tests," the starchy clerk told them.

As in a dream Florette followed another uniform out to Pop's truck and climbed in when he opened the door for her. "Now you sit still a minute and get your breath." — He was laughing as if in response to the silly grin which she could feel still stretching her mouth. "Was it so bad as all that? Now take her along this block and turn left so you can go over to Sixteenth."

She let in the clutch with a rude scrape that cleared away the rosy mists. Right lane: it would be right lane.

"Now," the examiner continued, "suppose you're going to the Five-and-Dime. Bring her in at that meter."

The space was almost too short, and if this had been a mean man, Florette would have thought he was trying to spoil things for her. But he wasn't mean. Florette steered parallel to the car in front of the parking space indicated, backed in with a good, swift turn, and straightened out.

"Swell," the examiner said. "Now to the next corner and turn left onto Main."

She was able to smile knowingly. "Can't turn left there, sir."

"Well, blessed if you aren't right!" he exclaimed, his mouth quirking with approval.

"Swell driver," he reported when they returned.

The patrolman was still there. "I already knew that," he said. "But remember, young lady: no more speeding!"

Fred followed Florette into the office. "This guy's okay," his mentor said. Florette felt an ungenerous glow. Fred was okay, but she was swell.

Miss Sansome looked as pleased as if it were she who was being handed the crisp new receipts — temporary licenses — in exchange for the five-dollar bill she had lent the two. "Why don't we throw a party to celebrate? My treat. Potter's maple walnut parfait?"

"It's keen — and their most expensive number." Eloquently Fred licked his lips.

In the drugstore Florette silently spooned in the ravishing blend of ice cream, whipped cream, fruity syrup and nuts. Joy had flooded her too full for words, even without this luscious confection. It was only as the three of them searched for the last fragments of nut that she spoke breathlessly.

"Something funny — You know the time I flunked. That time I'd — asked — asked Him to help me. I never did pray so hard." She kept her eyes lowered in embarrassment. "Honest, I thought He would. But He never."

"And you asked him again this time?" Miss Sansome said.

"No'm. This time I never asked Him nothing. And look."

"Didn't you ever think He had different ways of helping?" Miss Sansome's voice was thoughtful. "That He might send people to help? Like Jane Brown. And Fred. And me."

Florette drew a quick breath. "You think that? Honest?"

"Well, doesn't it figure?"

Fred cleared his throat uncomfortably. "Sure thank you for the treat, Miss Sansome. I'll bring my two twenty-five tomorrow."

Fred bade them goodbye when they left the drugstore.

He would take his father's car to the shop and tell him the good news — "Bum, am I?" — and then wait to ride home with him. Florette and Miss Sansome climbed into the truck again and drove back to the dump house.

"This time I won't go in," Miss Sansome said. "More fun to tell them yourself."

"You're so good!" Florette said. "Oh, you're the best!"

Pop roared at her as soon as she opened the door. "Now what the tarnation was all this? That Mrs. Sansome is a smooth one, but I wouldn't put anything past a dog-lover like her. What you been up to?"

Dropping down on a chair, Florette waved the receipt at him. "I took the test again."

He gaped at the slip of paper. "You didn't pass it?"

She nodded triumphantly. "So did Fred."

"Oh, him. Squeaked through by the skin of your teeth, I reckon. What mark did you get on the question part?"

"Ninety-six." Florette tried to keep her voice casual, but it broke in two in the middle of the ninety-six.

"Who you kidding?"

"Ask Miss Sansome. Ask Fred Barlow."

"What did that young punk get? One hundred and ten?"

"Ninety. But I've passed, Pop. I've passed."

Pop clapped shut his hanging mouth. "About time," he said.

147

14

THE NEXT day was Saturday and Florette took out the truck by herself, to pick up a regular weekly load. She wore jeans and one of Pop's work shirts. First she wrapped a scarf around her head, but a look in the glass made her rummage round for an old stocking cap that hid all her hair without looking so girlish.

"Now anybody'd take me for a boy," she said hopefully.

"Hmph," said Mom.

Driving by herself and knowing she had a perfect right to — it was wonderful. It put her on top of the world. She had been to this house with Pop, and her mind had a way of mapping out a route and keeping the map in her memory.

She still felt lighter than air as she swung the cans of trash to her shoulder, jogged out with them, emptied them into the truck. The garbage, to be sure, was not especially pleasant. The tin cans were easy, especially here, where they were always washed and flattened. Florette thought the woman must be a perfect housekeeper, since she was so particular about her cans.

In the miscellaneous trash there was a gray plush

148

elephant which Florette carefully set aside. It was clean, and when she had sewed up the little rip in its back, so that Elvie couldn't pull out the stuffing, it would make him a nice toy, and she could use it in telling him an elephant story. It seemed like a good-luck omen that she should find something special for Elvie on her very first trip alone.

The elephant was not her only good luck. She went to the kitchen door to tell the woman that she had finished, hoping that since it was the fourth load they had hauled for her, she would have the five dollars ready. Some women were seldom at home, and others seldom had the money on hand.

This time the payment was ready and the woman said, "You're the daughter, aren't you? Will you tell your father that the people next door have a load for him today?"

"Thank you, ma'am, I'll go right over. I'm alone today, but I'm real strong."

It was exhilarating to hand Pop a little wad of paper money when she got home.

"We can pay the phone bill," he said, stuffing the roll into his old wallet. "I got an order that will take the both of us this afternoon, and I'll stop by and pay that dang bill."

"You well enough, Pop? Sure?"

"Yeah. Feel better today."

The load was a big one, with tree branches and a

heavy burnt-out incinerator. Pop got six dollars for it. But when he stopped at the telephone company he found the business office closed for the weekend. He would have to wait till Monday, and that would mean more days without a telephone.

Unwillingly Florette suggested that they drive around and look for loads, as he had done before.

"I can run in and ask," she offered, though she hated to go to people's back doors. Still, they were far enough from home so that she was unlikely to run into any of her schoolmates. And in this way they did get one load, and two orders for Monday.

Pop was tired, and Florette could tell that his back was painful, though she had done most of the lifting. "We'll put for home now," he said. "Might pick up some hamburger on the way. But look, Florrie, how's about your stopping downtown and getting you a dress? How much would it be, one that wouldn't let go all the buttons and seams first time you washed it?"

"They have real good ones for five-six dollars." Florette caught her breath at the thought. Then she shook a reluctant head. "Pop, couldn't we get that house paint instead? I can wash that best dress real careful, and iron it a little, even if it is drip-dry. A while longer. But we'd ought to get that paint on. The Man from the Rehab — anyway, the man to see Elvie might come, and —"

Pop stepped on the gas. "Drat the man. What

150

business is it of his? Drat that teacher. Drat you, Florette Cochrane, sticking your oar into what ain't your business."

Florette sat silent and pulled together as if she could keep from sticking out and getting hurt. After a while Pop slowed down and looked sidewise at her.

"You ain't such a bad kid, Florrie. Maybe you couldn't help it, oncet they seen Elvie. But your pop's plumb pooped. How'd the dratted paint get onto the dratted house if we did buy it?"

"Oh, Pop, I could do it. I could work a couple hours tonight, the days are so long. Oh, Pop, there's a paint store right next to the corner of Sixteenth and Main — Right here, Pop."

He pulled out his wallet and thrust several bills at her. "Okay. You win," he said, drawing up to the curb before the store. "Hyper in and make this go as far as you can."

They stopped again, at a little old grocery that crouched behind an old-fashioned boardwalk with a wooden canopy. "Get more for your money at a place like this. Who you reckon pays for all the shiny glass and nickel in them soopers?" Pop asked. "You buy two pounds," he said firmly, "and some of that shell macaroni and a big can of tomatoes. This outdoor air has give me an appetite, first time in a coon's age. And macaroni and meatballs is one thing your mom can do real good. Might heave her out of her rocker."

151

Florette hardly waited for the truck to stop before she was out and dashing into the house, hugging her bag of groceries in both arms because it was weak and splitting at the bottom.

"Mom," she wheedled, "Pop's mouth's watering for your macaroni and meatballs, and here's all the makings."

"Now what you got up your sleeve, Florrie Cochrane? Trying to sneak out of cooking? You know good and well how faint it turns me to work over a coal fire."

"They had a special on that strawb'ry jam you like so good," said Florette, already pulling on a pair of Pop's worst overalls. "I'm going to start in on this paint job." She was outside before Mom could make further objections.

She brought the paint cans from the truck, and the best of the scrubby brushes from where she had hidden them under the house, and squatted down to stir the paint richly. She was interrupted by a demanding wail from Elvie, pushing against the bulging screen door.

"Coral!" Florette shouted, in a tone she seldom used toward her sister. "Kindly look after Elvie till suppertime."

She did not stop to see whether Coral was complying. She did not need to. The change from Elvie's demanding call to his protesting shriek told her that Coral had grabbed him up. The shriek steadied to a continuous howl as Florette marched around to the front of the house and began to slap on the glorious white paint. This time she knew that there was at least enough for one side, and it seemed only sensible to start with the wall that would make the most impression on a visitor. She was laying on the whiteness with joyous speed when Coral stamped toward her, Elvie on one hip and the playpen trundling ahead of her.

"This dumb kid won't do a thing I tell him," Coral snapped. "He's spoiled rotten and it's your fault, Florette Cochrane." She rolled the playpen as close to Florette as she could, and thumped Elvie down inside it.

"You give me a pain," Florette told her retreating sister. "No, no, not you, Elvie baby. You're Florrie's little angel. And it's you Florrie's doing this for, so the Man won't think we're just trash."

Talking and singing to the child, she went on painting while the good smell of meatballs from the house made her mouth water and her empty stomach feel emptier.

The macaroni dish was good, and everyone ate heartily, even Coral, though she slapped pettishly at the flies and complained that it was dangerous to have so many, and for goodness sake couldn't they get screens?

Florette had left on the overalls, now splashed with white, and the minute she finished eating she grabbed Elvie and made for the door. "Coral, suppose you wash up for once," she suggested.

"Well, who was your servant last year?" Coral retorted.

Pop seldom paid any attention to the girls' bickering, but this time he roared at his younger daughter, spatting the oilcloth with an angry palm. "You do like your sister says. Florrie put in a good hard day and now she's got a right to do what she wants to."

Thankfully Florrie escaped to do what she wanted to, picking up the elephant on the way, though she had not yet mended it. "Elvie be ree-eal careful," she said, "Don't hurt the poor little efelant."

When she had deposited him in the pen and the toy on his lap, he managed to get his arms around the elephant and make kissing sounds toward its head. He was asleep before darkness forced Florette to stop.

The next day was Sunday, and Florette was at the painting as soon as it was light. "That last stretch is pretty doggone thin," Pop said, sitting on an upended box in the sun to watch her work. "But another week or so, if things keep up good, we can get enough for the second coat."

Dripping with sweat in the hot sun, Florette pushed back her hair with the curve of her elbow and gloated over her work. "You reckon you could nail in a new board on the porch floor, Pop?" she asked. "I don't think I could do it good enough."

Maybe if once Pop got the hammer in his hand he might have a hankering to nail up some other loose places. But Florette had learned from experience that she'd better not say any more. She left him sitting in the May sunshine while she flew at the everlasting scrubbing of the floor, and the sweeping and shaking of a few strips of rag carpeting that had come on a load. After an hour of her dashing in and out with doors banging, Pop rose, straightened up with a prodigious yawning stretch, and hobbled in to look for the hammer and nails.

By the time darkness fell, Florette had done all she could to make the place decent. She had besides heated water and washed Elvie's most presentable rompers, and other necessaries for him and for herself. "I shall scream," said Coral, "if I see that same dress of yours hanging on our lines again. And there won't be any color left in it."

"Mmmm," Florette said noncommittally, and then, "Mmmm" again, as she slid into her pallet at last and pulled up sheet and quilt against the cool freshness of the night air. She stretched her arms above her head and sighed with contented weariness.

Coral had come in and was undressing, dropping her clothes in their customary ring around her feet. "I suppose you didn't think to wash anything for me, Florrie?" she asked.

"I did not, Coral Cochrane," Florette said through a satisfying yawn. "You had plenty time to wash your own duds."

"It wouldn't have been much more work while you were at it, and you know how I get eczema when I wash."

"I've heard about it," Florette said pleasantly, "but I have yet to see it. Red hands, yes, but take a look at mine if you want to see red hands. What with turpentine to get off the paint, and lye for scrubbing the floor — but, anyway, the place smells cleaner. And it looks a little bit cleaner — "

"Ve-ry little, if you ask me. It looks like a junkshop, and that's about all it is. Oh, you don't know what it's like to want to be somebody, Florette Cochrane, and never have any chance at all. You don't know — " Her words trailed off in angry sobbing.

"Just why don't I know?" Florette demanded. "I'm human, too, though you don't seem to think so." But her quick anger ebbed as quickly, and she said sleepily, "You just wait. Us Cochranes are on our way . . ." With the words, she slipped into deep, sweet slumber.

15

FLORETTE slept long and hard, and wakened only when Elvie came crawling in and rained wet kisses on her face.

"Mercy to us!" she cried, grabbing him and leaping up to estimate the time by the height of the sun. "Looks like I could sleep all day."

She did take a minute, as soon as she had dressed, to circle the outside of the house, sniffing the good paint smell and beaming at the way the fresh surface caught the light. Pop followed her around, thumbs hooked in the top of his overalls.

"But that old wood drinks it in and begs for more," Florette complained. "It's only a little less dried out than the roof."

Pop backed off, peering under the peak of his cap at the curling shingles. "Well," he said, "long's it don't rain — "

Florette whirled past him and into the house, keeping back the remarks that tingled on her tongue. Poor Pop. After all, that back of his was a real hurt, not like Coral's eczema.

"Mom," she said as she alternately sipped coffee and

made sandwiches for her lunch and Coral's, "don't wear that best romper on Elvie. I kind of want to keep it for when the Man comes."

"That man," Mom scolded. "That man ain't ever going to show up, Florrie, and that's sure soon enough for me."

If he were to come even today, Florette thought despairingly — In the bright morning sun it looked as if all the scrubbing and lye had done was to make the ancient stains stand out. What was it they looked like? Like freckles when a person's face went pale. But worst of all were the window shades, ragged, faded, greasy. With an exclamation of disgust, Florette ran and rolled each one to the top. She had to do it by hand, because the springs didn't work.

"All that sun in here," Pop joked, "and you'll fade the wall-to-wall carpets. Besides showing up them strubbly curtains."

"Pop — " Florette granted his joke an appreciative chuckle and admitted to herself that washing and starching the curtains was her next job — "Pop, the porch sure looks keen without that hole in the floor."

"What you buttering me up for now? Better shake a leg, girls. If that clock ain't crazy you got to get going."

" 'Oh, what a beautiful morning,' " sang Florette, picking Elvie up for a bear hug. " 'Oh, what a beautiful day!' "

She did feel that there was some truth in the song as

she strode along the road that Monday morning. She darted out from it to pick stems of drooping blue bells with pink buds, and a fragrant cluster of late sand lilies, and some small, starry white flowers. She would take them to Miss Sansome, though it might be more sensible to give them to her look-down-the-nose English teacher. The idea went against the grain. It was different, buttering up Pop. He kind of needed it. And, besides, it sometimes worked.

Miss Sansome greeted the wildflowers appreciatively. "Mertensia or Languid Lady," she said of the drooping bells. "And sand lilies and Spring Beauties, of course. The Johnny-Jump-Ups ought to be in bloom, too. You look happy, Florette."

Florette hunched her shoulders, hugging herself. "Things are kind of on the up-and-up at our house. But, Miss Sansome, is there any way I could know when the Man is fixing to come and see Elvie? Mom's kind of edgewise about it, and Pop doesn't like it too well, either. So it would be good for me to be there when the Man comes."

It seemed unnecessary to explain that she needed to be there to scrub Elvie and get him into clean rompers.

"Why, yes." Miss Sansome eyed her thoughtfully as if reading her mind. "I'll phone Mr. Argon and ask him to check with me. Everything else is all right, then?"

Some of the brightness drained out of the sky. "I don't guess I'm going to pass. Miss Orfut says not."

"Let me go with you and talk to Miss Orfut," Miss

Sansome suggested. "But first, will you please get some water for the flowers, in this vase? It looks right for them, don't you think?"

Florette nodded, admiring the little pottery vase, with blue and green in it, blending like the rose and gray and green in her cracked one. She filled it at the nearest hall fountain. Wouldn't it be nice if they could get water at home just by turning a handle? She was back in a moment, and watching Miss Sansome arrange the delicate sprays.

"I want to see if Miss Orfut and I can't cook up some way to give you a lift with your studies," Miss Sansome said, almost as if she were talking to herself. "A girl who can pass the driver's examination with a grade of ninety-six!"

In Miss Orfut's room she repeated those words. Miss Orfut lifted incredulous brows and stared at Florette as if she were trying to see something that wasn't there.

"I'd faint if she ever got ninety-six in my class," she said bluntly. "Constance, her grades aren't even border-line. And I've talked to her other teachers. Art and Home Ec and Gym are the only ones where she's passing."

Florette's face grew hot and her hands bigger and bigger. Miss Sansome reached over and patted her.

"But it doesn't make sense," she said. "She's so extra quick with machines. And has that phenomenal memory. Yes, I know her reading is poor, and almost everything in school depends more or less on books. Remedial reading just must be the key."

"With the teaching load I have, Constance," Miss Orfut said, flushing, "I can't see how I can add remedial reading for one girl, especially one who came in the middle of the semester." (One stupid girl, Florette thought she wanted to say.) "Remedial reading is a science in itself, as you well know. And, anyway, I doubt if it is the answer. She's far past the age when reversal is likely. I've watched for that tendency. But you know there are minds — "

"Yes, some minds are tuned to books and others to things," Miss Sansome put in hastily, as if afraid that the other teacher would say too much. "If only we had those vocational courses going — Well, time for the bell."

Linking arms with Florette, she trotted her briskly out of the room. "Don't worry too much, honey. Do your durndest and we'll see if we can't come up with something."

At the close of the school day Miss Sansome detained her. "You still look worried. Want to stop and talk it out with me?"

"Oh, I'd love it. But Pop has extra heavy loads today, and I got to make tracks so I can help him."

"Well, why don't I run you home? — No, I'll be gaining more than you will. You can listen to my engine, Dr. Cochrane, and tell me if there's a kind of knock in it. And if the faithful swain is waiting, we can give him a lift, too."

Funny how nice it was to have somebody to be teased about.

Stopping in front of the dump house, Miss Sansome said, "Why, you've begun to paint! Makes quite a change."

"Yes'm."

"It's Flor did it," Fred bragged. "Isn't she a whizz? My folks would have heart failure if I started anything like that."

"Soon as — soon as I can I'll put on another coat," Florette murmured. "It'll look a lot whiter then."

Yet in contrast to the dingy shades it looked startlingly white already. "Oh, Mom went and pulled down the blinds," Florette blurted out. "They're the ones was up when we got here."

Miss Sansome struck her hands together. "What a pity! I just changed to venetian blinds in my living room. And the ones I took down were so good — almost like new — I hated to throw them out. There were only three, to be sure."

Florette's breath quickened, but she said nothing. She mustn't let Miss Sansome or Fred think she was asking for handouts.

"I don't suppose — " Miss Sansome hesitated — "you'd want to bother to investigate them, Florette? I'd be thankful to get my rubbish hauled away, if your father isn't too busy. And then you might just take a

162

look and see if they were good enough — ”

"I'd be pleased to look at them," Florette said primly.

"I'm afraid they're the wrong size — ”

"But they could easy be cut down and fastened to the right-size rollers," said Florette.

"By a smart person they could," agreed Miss Sansome, making a compliment out of the words.

When Florette and Pop picked up that load, the last on their way home, Florette found in it a bundle of beige-colored shades, tied securely together, and happily set them in a corner of the truck where they would not be soiled by any of the rubbish. Home at last, she ran into the house with them and untied them.

"Now where did those drop from?" asked Pop, hobbling in and letting himself down in a chair.

"Off the load." Joy surged through Florette as she fingered them and sniffed their clean fragrance. "These're not paper. They're cloth."

"Don't fit no windows we got."

"But I can cut them down."

"The good stuff folks throw out," Pop said sourly. "Looks like things is awful uneven in this world."

"Yes, isn't it?" Florette answered amiably, running to take down one of the ragged shades and spread it on the floor.

She had a full evening's work, first marking around the old shades, with a two-by-four as a ruler to make the penciled lines straight, and then cutting with painful care. She was running the shears through the fine, firm

163

cloth, tongue between teeth and breath held, when Elvie came creeping and rolling over to her. With gurgling triumph he flung himself upon her, making the shears jerk and slash the shade.

"Mercy to us, Elvie!" she cried. "Look what you made me do!"

Amazement filled Elvie's small face. All its softness puckered into crying, and he howled and hiccuped and strangled on his sobs.

Remorsefully Florette pulled him into her arms. "There, there! Sister was nasty and horrid. There, there!"

"Coral!" bellowed Pop. "Looks like you could leastways get up the gumption to keep Elvie offen Florrie while she's working like she is."

It was Coral's turn to look astonished.

"You slipped out of doing a hand's turn this whole day," Pop went on. "Seen you putting for home when me and Florrie was hauling the last load. Where'd you been, young lady?"

"Oh, out around," Coral mumbled through the plastic roller which she held in her mouth while she wrapped a silky bright strand of hair around another. "One of the kids gave me a lift and we went downtown and sort of window-shopped."

"What kind of curlers are those?" Mom asked sleepily. "Where'd you get them?"

"These? Oh, Jane Brown."

"Jane never curls her hair," Florette objected. She

was still comforting Elvie, who had forgivingly settled against her, thumb in mouth. Over his head she looked with sharpened question at her sister.

"Don't I know it, smarty?" Coral retorted. "That's why she gave them to me. Came with some shampoo she bought at the Dime Store."

"She give you those little combs with the bows on them?"

"She didn't like those, either, once she got them out of the store," Coral said airily.

"I can't feature her picking out such junk in the first place." A vague uneasiness plagued Florette, but right now she could not stop to figure it out. She had to get Elvie into dry clothes and tuck him into bed and then finish her evening's project.

When she had all three of the smooth, good-smelling shades the right size, and the wooden slats at the bottom sawed off and replaced, there remained the tacking on to the old rollers.

"Have to use real little tacks, so they'll roll good," Pop advised. "Might be enough in that tin lid on top of the cupboard. I pick out the good nails and such as that from the trash."

It was prickly work to rummage out enough that were the right size or nearly the right size, but at last she had the three shades firmly attached. Pop stopped her when she ran to put one up.

"If you want 'em to pull down and snap back like they're supposed to," he contributed helpfully, "you got to wind the spring real tight. Fetch it here and I'll show you."

When he had turned it over and over, it unwound with a whirr and gave his fingers a vicious snap. "You see how it goes," he said, handing it back to her.

Florette's fingers suffered the same punishment. With an exasperated snort, she tried winding with an old fork and using it to hold the tightened spring steady till she could slip it into its slot.

"Florrie, you got brains in your fingers."

"But none in her head." Coral was still sulking over Pop's rebuke.

"Guess you got yours in your fingernails and hair," Florette told her, hopping on a shaky chair and balancing there as she put up the shade.

"Not half bad," Pop admitted, when all three were hung, the one jagged edge as inconspicuous as possible. "What did I tell you gals? This house won't look so worse when I get time to fix it up. Paint in all these rooms and lonillion on the floor — "

"You got the middle blind crooked," Coral said.

"Fix it yourself if it looks so bad to you," Florette answered. It really was crooked, but right now she was too tired to bear the thought of climbing up and taking it down again. When it was rolled as high as it would go —

Wouldn't it be wonderful if the Man were to come tomorrow! Florette refrained from speaking her unpopular wish aloud.

16

ALL NEXT day Florette hoped that Miss Sansome would beckon her and say that the Man would be out that afternoon. But she didn't, and more days passed.

As far as school was concerned, they were worrisome days for Florette. Her reading was little better, though she had never before tried so hard. In some ways Miss Orfut's class was even worse, as if Miss Orfut felt that she ought to be doing something different for Florette, but didn't know what to do. The other classes were slightly improved, since Florette was listening more intently to what teachers and classmates said, reminding herself of her phe-nom-e-nal memory and trying to use it. To her surprise, Social Studies were sometimes interesting.

"You know," she said to Fred as they walked homeward one afternoon, "I always thought this automation was something brand-new. Looked like it was just sent to plague us. But that Socks teacher says they've had it one way or another, forever and ever. That Industrial Revolution in England — and how many folks lost their jobs when some guy invented machines to spin thread — and a machine to pick the seeds out of cotton."

"Gosh," Fred teased, "you going highbrow on me?"

She smiled, half pleased but half wishing Fred liked to talk about things. You couldn't expect everything, though. She tried again. "Honest, Fred, it makes you feel kind of different, knowing that folks — other folks — have gone through it and come out all right after a while. That Socks teacher says that every generation has had them that called the inventions a plain curse, and others that called them a blessing."

"Yeah," Fred agreed. "You reckon you could give me a hand with a carburetor I bought off a junkman?"

"Sure," Florette agreed absently. It would be nice if she could tell Fred what else she had been thinking: that it had made her feel better about God, because likely He had to go slow or the world would get worse snarled up than ever. But of course you couldn't very well talk to any boy about God. It would seem kind of indecent.

She couldn't talk to Fred about Coral, either, though she worried about her sister, with a pricking, nagging anxiety. Coral was always dawdling home late, with no explanation, or else with stories about stopping at Jane's house or going downtown. And when Florette tidied their room — still expecting the Man — she found things she did not understand: a necklace, a bracelet, a handbag, all looking brand-new. When she questioned her sister about them, Coral flew into a rage. What business was it of Florette's if Coral's friends liked her so well they wanted to give her presents? And if Florette meant to sneak around and tattle to Pop and Mom — well, two could play at that game, Coral guessed.

"That's okay by me," Florette retorted, "as long as you don't tell them some of those whoppers of yours."

It was almost the end of May when Miss Sansome gave Florette the long-awaited message. "Mr. Argon telephoned that he could come and see Elvie today. He'll meet you here, so that you can ride with him and show him the way. It looks like rain, so it may be a help to ride instead of walk."

Florette's heart, lifting with excited hope, sagged again as she looked out at the ominous sky. Maybe, though, the storm would fool them once more. It hadn't rained all month except for sprinkles that did little more than give the air a nice smell. If you had those heavy dark clouds in Nebraska, you could count on a drenching downpour, but here, so close to the mountains, they often scooted past without letting down a drop.

When a tremendous deluge stretched silvery screens of rain across all the windows, and as suddenly began to hammer them with hail, Florette remembered the leaky roof, which Pop had not yet mended, since the drought had continued to make mending unnecessary. And there were the broken windows that would douse those new shades.

She was almost stifled with eagerness and worry when

at dismissal time the Man came into her homeroom.

In Florette's mind the Man had grown increasingly tall and broad and handsome, because it seemed as if it would take that kind to work the wonders she hoped for. Instead, he was thin and small, his eyes below the level of Florette's, and thick-lensed glasses making them into strange blue-green marbles. Yet those marbles were at once probing and kind.

All the way home he talked to Florette about this and that. Often he paused as if for responses, but he had few from his companion. Her mind was too busy racing ahead to the house.

One of her fears was realized when they drew up before it. The truck was parked there, so Pop was probably at home.

She motioned the Man to go up the steps and in at the door, calling ahead of him, "Mom! Pop! Here is the gentleman."

Mutely she gestured toward a chair, surprisingly enough empty of any rubbish.

"This is my mother," she stammered, finding her voice. "And my father. This is the gentleman we've been expecting. Will you excuse me while I see to my little brother?"

There were good points along with the bad, she thought as she carried Elvie out to the kitchen. She could see Mom hastily pushing back a straggle of hair and fumbling to fasten a button that had come undone. And Mom had left the clean rompers in the drawer where Florette had put them. It didn't take long to give Elvie a quick scrub in the dishpan, though he gasped and whimpered at the chill of the water. Glancing out at the living room as she buttoned Elvie up, she noticed that her mother had mopped the floor and spread newspapers down to keep the mud from tracking in.

But the proud new shade at one broken window showed a long smear, not only wet but stained from the old roof, while at another the hopefully starched old curtain hung limp and discouraged. And on the newspapered floor stood pans and buckets, the recently emptied ones tinkling musically as they caught some of the drip from the roof. Florette looked out just in time to see Mr. Argon jerk back his head as a drop splashed on his nose.

Pop said, "If you'd hitch your chair a mite this way, mister — Sorry you found us so messed up. That hail pounded our roof to a fare-ye-well."

Florette winked at Pop behind their caller's back. Pop was making out that their leaks were brand-new.

"Yes sir, I got to climb up and nail on some shingles, soon's it dries off," Pop went on. "Maybe Florrie here will have to do it. Purt' near the man of the house, Florrie's had to be since this here sacred iliac's took me so bad."

"Sacred iliac: that's clever. I like a man with a sense of humor, Mr. Cochrane," the Man said, throwing back his head to laugh.

Pop quickly covered his look of bewilderment with

171

a polite grin, but Florette felt herself flushing. She had wondered about that sacred business. Maybe Pop had got the words mixed.

Hurriedly she roached Elvie's fluff of curls high with the wet brush, and then carried him out and stood before the Man. "This is him," she said. "This is my little brother."

"Me and his mom, we feel real sorry to have you waste your time coming so far," said Pop. "Like you see, there ain't no manner of use. It ain't little Elvie's fault he ain't got good sense. He'll have a home as long as we live, and as long as Florrie does."

"But Elvie has got sense," Florette burst out. "It's just that it's inside him and he can't get it out. Look, mister — " She reached for the toy elephant and sat down, hooking her toes behind the chair rungs, so that she could more securely hold Elvie and the toy. With a shyly apologetic glance at her caller, she began one of her stories.

"Listen, Elvie: this little efelant, he comes walking along — Now, listen to Sister, Elvie; the Man won't hurt you. He's not used to strangers, mister — Now listen, Elvie; the efelant comes walk-walk-walking onto Elvie's little hand. And then he comes walk-walk-walking up Elvie's little arm. And then he comes — jumpity-jump! — right into Elvie's little neck. And kisses him!"

The magic of the story had drawn Elvie's attention away from the alarming Mr. Argon. When the elephant landed in his neck he doubled up with laughter.

172

"Way it looks to me — " Florette's voice was husky but positive — "he wouldn't think it was funny if he didn't have some sense."

"He laughs because he's ticklish." Pop's tone was as positive as his daughter's.

"But he laughs at the right places in all my stories."

Mr. Argon's eyes behind those thick glasses were intent on the child. "I believe Miss Cochrane has some reason for thinking as she does. Would he let me take him?" From his pocket he pulled a gaily colored rattle that played a tune when he wound it. "Come on over, Elvie, and you can make it sing, too."

Wide eyes fixed on the enticing toy, Elvie huddled closer to Florette.

"He's plumb took up with Florrie," Pop apologized.

"Anyone can see she's good to him. And good for him. And he needs to have somebody think he's wonderful, even more than the rest of us do. Pretty little fellow. Was he born that way, or was it some later injury?"

"Doc said his oxygen was cut off by the way he come," Pop said. "I don't know. She had an extra hard time, and Doc hurried things much as he could. For quite some time we thought that Son was making it okay."

While he kept the tune playing over and over, Mr. Argon studied the delicate small face.

"Nothing like that happened with our first." Pop's voice creaked, and he kept his eyes away from Florette.

"To make her — different, I mean. But I tell Florrie she's got brains in her fingers, even if she was behind the door when they were passing out the sense."

Florette flushed and pretended not to hear.

"And in her heart, too," Mr. Argon said surprisingly.

Pop's eyes softened as they occasionally did when they regarded her: occasionally but not often. "Mister, you got something there. Couldn't nobody ask for a bigger heart. But our Coral," he went on, "she never had a thing wrong. Pretty as a posy, if I do say so, and smart. Hardly opens her books for homework, but passes ever' time. Ever see our Coral?"

Mr. Argon nodded absently. "Miss Sansome pointed her out to me. An unusually pretty girl. But I thought she was your niece."

Pop snorted. "That's a fancy story Coral's cooked up. Don't ask me why. We're the only pop and mom she ever had. She's too big for her britches, that girl."

The Man seemed to dismiss Coral from his thoughts. "We shall have to approach the child differently, I see. How would it be if you read him a story, Miss Florette, and got his attention that way?"

Again he was fishing in a side pocket. This time he produced a small book and handed it to Florette, who took it uneasily. When she had opened it, above Elvie's top curl, she shook her head. "The words are too long. And when the print is so small — "

"You see, mister?" Pop was nervously knocking out his pipe on the newspaper at his feet. "Me and Mom,

174

we ain't what you'd call brainy, but we can read a sight better than Florrie can."

"How is it, Florette?" Mr. Argon's voice was kindly. "Miss Sansome says your eyes are practically normal."

"Yes'm — yessir. I see okay." Florette's mouth trembled, and Elvie put up an uncertain hand toward it, his face pitiful. "It looks like — like the letters jump around so — "

Pop laughed. " 'Tain't good enough, Florrie."

"But that's how it is," persisted Florette, opening up as she had never done before, because the question in the Man's eyes was so interested and gentle. "And seems as if the wrong end of the line is the right end and that makes — a mixup."

Mr. Argon patted her shoulder. He didn't say anything. What was there to say? Except that she was just extra dumb.

"Well, then, why don't we try another way?" He reached into a briefcase he had set on the floor beside him and produced some papers. "Let's make out I'm giving you a test, Florette. That would take the pressure off Elvie. You don't mind, do you?"

"Anything that would help Elvie." But she looked suspiciously at the papers. Teachers had sometimes tested her with papers, though nothing had come of it.

Mr. Argon continued as if he hadn't noticed her doubt. While Elvie leaned against his sister's breast, clutching the musical toy, the Man asked all kinds of questions. Since she was hearing them instead of trying

175

to read, she could figure most of them out. She spoke slowly and quietly, not to frighten the child, and twined his top curl around her finger, again and again, with a soothing rhythm.

It seemed a long while before the Man finished, making little marks on his papers as he spoke. By that time Florette had rewound the toy, and Elvie was giggling at the music.

Without comment, Mr. Argon drew a bright red monkey from his briefcase, and lifted Elvie over to his knee. Talking, he worked the monkey's mechanism for minutes on end, Florette's eyes busy with the man's face and the child's. When Pop had shaken out his pipe again, he said huskily, "Not a thing to be done for the poor little feller, I reckon."

"On the contrary," said Mr. Argon. Florette took a deep breath. "I think it extremely likely that he is both trainable and educable. "Wait!" he cautioned, at Florette's joyful gasp. "He won't ever walk like a normal child, or speak like one. But unless I'm greatly mistaken, he can be taught to get around, perhaps with leg braces, and to dress himself and go to the bathroom. And taught to speak so you can understand him — "

"And read?" begged Florette.

Those small blue-green eyes were especially kind as they studied her eager face. "I think so. Definitely I think so. It will take time, and the work of people who have been trained in that kind of teaching."

Mom threw her apron over her head and rocked to and

176

fro, moaning. Questioningly the man stared at her.

"Mister," said Pop, "with all due respect, we don't want Elvie to be took away by nobody, no time, nowheres. We're poor folks, but we love our kids, and we aim to take care of them as good as we know how."

"Your attitude is thoroughly understandable, Mr. Cochrane, but it is based on a misunderstanding. We don't suggest taking Elvie away, except as your two daughters go away, to school in the morning and home in the afternoon. There's a school within driving distance — " He glanced at the truck, parked in sight of the window. "It's too late to go there today, but I'll stay over, and tomorrow I'll take you all to see for yourselves."

It was just then, when Florette's heart was swelling with joy almost to the bursting point, that the telephone rang.

With Elvie astride her hip, Florette ran to answer it. "Hello," she said, and then stared frowningly at the receiver, for Coral was speaking to her, in a voice that was strained and unnatural.

"Florrie, you and Pop have to come down to the Town Hall right away. You know where it is — " Her words were almost lost in an angry sob.

"But — why are you at the Town Hall, Corrie?"

"Oh, skip it, can't you? Just get down here quick and ask for — " Her voice turned away from the phone a minute — "ask for the police court. Oh, Florrie, hurry up!"

17

A CONFUSED and frightened half hour followed the phone call.

Mr. Argon gathered up his things, saying he would be back after school next day. Pop bade him an absent-minded goodbye, and Florette went to the door with him. Thoughtfully he studied her face.

"It's the pretty sister?"

Florette nodded, not trusting herself to speak.

"Remember, she probably has her problems, too," he said gently.

The rain had stopped, and soon Florette and Pop were sloshing through puddles on the highway, and then throwing up bright spray from pavements already drying in Colorado's hot sunshine.

"I don't get it," Pop groaned. "What's she got herself into?"

"She never said," Florette answered for the tenth time. "But it's bad trouble. You could tell from her voice."

"Kids! Looks like they's no end to the trouble they can rake up these days. And they don't have a lick of respect for their elders. Coral, she's so — so good-looking. You don't reckon one of them high-flying fellers has taken advantage? If he has, I'll break his good-for-nothing neck for him — "

Florette's sigh shuddered through her whole body. "You can't prove nothing by me, Pop. She never tells me nothing. And you know yourself she's a couple hours getting home from school lots of days — "

"Seems like you could take some responsibility for your little sister," Pop growled.

Florette sniffed desperately and grabbed for a Kleenex that wasn't there.

"Oh, now now now. Don't take me too serious, Florrie." Pop's voice shook. "I know you got your hands full. Maybe more than a youngun should."

They parked beside the mall that stretched behind the municipal building. Florette had thought that structure grand and beautiful, with the grassy mall and the city park across the street from its entrance, and the mountain brook dashing between tall old trees at one side of it. Today it looked like a great beast, crouching to spring at the Cochrane family and tear away their self-respect — ragged, but all they had left to cover them.

Pop, his cap in his hand for once, as if deferring to the power of the law, huskily inquired where the police court was at. They were motioned into a small, well-filled room.

Behind the desk a grave-looking police officer presided. Stiffly seated in chairs before him were Carol [handwritten: Coral] and two other girls whom Florette recognized only as Phyllis and Janet, girls whom Coral was often with. At the back of the room, as if they had come in just ahead of Pop and Florette, stood two sleek women and a large man — a real rich one, thought Florette — who stared indignantly at the officer in charge, and at the patrolman stationed beside him.

"This detective," said the seated police officer, "was summoned by the management of Lane and Borden's Apparel Shop to arrest these three young ladies, who had been apprehended taking merchandise."

"But of course we have an account at Lane and Borden's," one of the women cried out.

"Your daughter was not purchasing, madam; she was shoplifting. Officer, you have with you the merchandise in question?"

"Yes sir." On the desk he placed a handbag, a pair of gloves, a glittering heap of costume jewelry.

"This is absurd," the large man exploded. "Phyllis, tell him you have an allowance large enough to buy anything you want. You would not have the least reason to —"

Phyllis's voice was muffled by her handkerchief. "It was only for kicks, Daddy. Can't anybody understand? It was just for kicks —"

The presiding officer tapped on the desk and everyone fell silent, even the father, whose face had gone the color of a boiled beet. He glared incredulously, as if for years no one had dared tap at him or in any other way rebuke him.

"These young ladies have all admitted taking the merchandise," the officer stated. "At this point they could be lodged in jail."

Florette covered her mouth with her hands, and both mothers gave horrified gasps.

"Instead, we are releasing them to you, the parents. You may take them home for the present."

"The present? What do you mean, the present?" the big man bellowed, while one of the women backed up against him for support.

"The next step is referral to the chief probation officer. Then it is out of the hands of this court. We have only the booking of them."

"The booking," Pop muttered. "Booked by police."

"But what would the probation officer do to my poor baby?" the other mother said, dabbing at her eyes and her pink nose with a handkerchief that wafted an exotic scent through the close room.

"That will be up to him, madam. He may refer her to the court for a hearing with Judge Holley. Or he may put her on probation, to report to him or his deputies at stated intervals."

"But they're only children," quavered Phyllis's mother.

"It's an outrage," her husband seconded her. "Out of all proportion —"

"Mr. Allen, this is a kind of misdemeanor that has been dealt with too lightly. Your daughter could be sent to the State Industrial School for this. And she is fifteen years old — " He glanced at papers before him — "old enough to know that she has been guilty of theft in taking this handbag. You are dismissed."

Out in the truck again Pop drove for a while in ominous silence, his lean jaw working. When he spoke it was in an unfamiliar voice, and he did not look at either girl.

"Cochranes has been poor folks. Never have known one to get rich. But one thing nobody could say against them. Not even their worst enemy. Nobody — " He spatted his hand hard on the horn — "nobody in his right mind could ever say we took what wasn't ourn. Stole. Not till today."

"It's mean to call it that, Pop!" Coral wailed. "It was only like a game. It was Phyl and Jan thought it up. They said we could do it so slick nobody could catch us — "

"Did it for kicks, did you?" Pop's voice broke out of control. "Did it for a thrill. Well, young lady, if you ain't old enough to have more sense than such as that, you ain't too old to get the thrill of a good licking. With your pop's belt, no less. And I don't mean maybe. Kicks!"

"I never said I did it for kicks," Coral cried hysterically. "They did, but not me. You don't know what it's like to be a girl and not have pretty things, not have anything—"

"Hush your yapping," her father said harshly. "Can you see your sister stealing because she didn't have pretty things to wear? Can you?"

"Oh—Florrie." Coral's tone scorched and then chilled her sister.

None of them spoke again until they reached the house and Pop stamped in ahead. Mom looked up and asked, "Now what was all this about, I'd like to know?"

"You'll know plenty soon. Right now I got some unfinished business to tend to. If you hadn't of spared the rod all these years, like the Good Book says—"

He reached into the bedroom and pulled something from a hook on the wall, then swung round on his heel. From his hand dangled a long, stout leather belt.

"No, Pop, no!" Coral screamed.

Gladness surged through Florette. Coral had it coming to her, and never had Coral got what she deserved.

Then she looked at her sister's face, gone soft and crumpled as Elvie's might, and at her child hands, shaking when she pushed them out toward Pop, who was striding toward her. And somehow Florette was standing in front of the smaller girl, facing Pop. "No, Pop," she whispered. "No."

Pop was beyond reasoning, his face white and his eyes hard and bright as blue stones. "Get outen my way,

183

Florrie. I ain't aiming to hurt you, but so help me — "

"No, Pop, not with the belt — "

He was near enough so that the sweep of his arm brought the buckle end hissing around and catching Florette on her bare legs. A quiver ran through her, but she did not move, and her arms were still spread to shield the weeping, gasping Coral.

Mom had heaved herself out of her chair and was pulling at Pop's arm. It fell of itself when he saw the blood running down Florette's leg. He let Mom take the belt, and he dropped into a chair and stared bleakly ahead of him, while Elvie reached out his arms toward Florette, with frightened cries.

"Florrie," Coral whispered, "Florrie."

Shaking her head as if ridding herself of cobwebs, Florette went to the sink, leaving a red trail behind her. She poured water into the basin and washed the blood from her leg, kept washing while the blood kept coming. Finally she gave it up and went outdoors to sit on Pop's special box till her body should stop trembling.

18

Pop went off to the tavern. Mom puttered around in a silence punctuated by almost inaudible moans and sighs.

"Florrie," she said at length, "if you take Elvie offen my hands, I'll fix some supper. Corrie can help. My land, though, you'd ought to stick some bandages on them cuts. They's a few left in the box on top of the cupboard."

Big help Corrie will be, Florette thought, glancing into their room as she applied the bandage strips. Coral lay face down on her pallet.

It was a relief to take Elvie and go striding out of the house that had grown poisonous with the fumes of fear and despair. The child nestled his face in her neck and was silent and still, subdued by the anger and unhappiness around him.

"Listen, little angel," his sister coaxed. "You know what? Elvie's maybe going to school, just like Florrie and Corrie."

Peering down, she could see an eye opening to fix itself on her face. He hasn't any idea what school is, Florette told herself, and that's because we haven't taken

185

the trouble to explain anything to him.

"Yes, Elvie will learn to talk. And to walk. See, Sister walks." She nodded toward her striding feet. "And Elvie is going to walk."

Elvie giggled inquiringly, as at one of her stories. Well, it would take time. He would have to come into it little by little. At the school they would know how to open his mind and direct his muscles. At the school! Briefly her thoughts were lifted free from what had befallen the Cochranes.

She turned off on a country road that meandered across the prairie. The air was sweet. Seemed sweeter than in Nebraska. In English class they had a poem that said it was sweeter because it was nearer to heaven.

So many things were getting good now. Florette could drive, and with her help maybe they could take in enough to fix things up nicer. And there was Elvie. Florette's heart felt like a joyful jelly when she thought what might be ahead for Elvie. She gave a little hop and skip that made him clutch tighter, laughing.

"Oh, what a beautiful evening!" she sang, "Oh, what a beautiful day!"

On that line she stopped. How could she forget, even for a minute, what that day had happened to Coral? If Coral had disgraced only herself; but, no, she had brought shame to the whole family. And if they should send her to Morrison, the State Industrial School — Clenching her teeth, Florette tried to close her mind against that threat.

And there was Pop, at the tavern again. And here was Florette, not going to pass —

As if he felt the change of mood, Elvie whimpered, and she called herself back to smile at him.

"Listen, Elvie. Listen at that meadowlark. You know something? He acts like he's got a nest pretty close, and he's trying to keep us from thinking about it. He sings a little bit nicer than they did on the farm. Listen." She pursed her lips and imitated the gurgling liquid song. "And there's other little birds. Some are finches, but Sister doesn't know if they've all got names."

The sun had dropped behind the mountains, and a little sighing breeze came up. The air brimmed over with songs and sweet smells and twitterings.

"Mercy to us," Florette exclaimed, "we got to get home to supper." Whirling round, she strode back to the house.

She and Elvie and Mom were the only ones who sat down to the meal. Pop was still at the tavern, and Coral answered Florette's call without turning her head on the pillow. "Not hungry. Anyway, not hungry for any of that junk."

"Suit yourself," Florette replied.

When Pop came home they were all abed, having taken the precaution of going early. It was soon evident that Pop was not in one of his belligerent moods, but bubbling over with foolish humor.

"Wake up! Wake up, you lazybones," he saluted them, as he fired his cap across the room and settled

187

himself in his favorite chair. "I got news for you. I'm about to set up in business. Me and Florette together. Yessir. Going to have a machine shop of my own. Why not? Just give me one good reason why not?" he asked argumentatively. "Who was it could fix up all the neighbors' autos when they was plain buffaloed? Who is it can take an auto offen the dump, a dead and buried auto, and get it to running smooth as butter? Who made a brand-new truck out of two that was in the junkyard? What d'you say, Florrie? Speak up, girl!"

"Sure thing, Pop," Florette agreed from her pallet. "Nobody smarter. Only you can't have a business here. You remember that baler and what they said about zones."

Pop mixed a snort with a laugh. "Sure I remember, Florrie. Them sons of guns, they don't want nobody to get ahead of them. But they can't make a monkey out of J. P. Cochrane. No sir. I'll set up on a piece of ground just outside city limits, where they can't touch me."

He was rubbing his hands together and throwing back his head to laugh. "No more of that down-your-nose talk from fat old biddies: 'Now, my man, see that you clean out all that trash real good,'" he mimicked. "No, sir, be my own man again. As for Miss Coral —" his voice changed abruptly — "you swipe anything again, Coral Cochrane, even bubble gum, and you'll see what's what. Your pop will get you out where there ain't no sister to pertect you. Have that pretty face scarred with a belt buckle and see how you like it. If they don't send you to Morrison, which by rights they'd ought to." Again his voice changed, this time filling itself with a savage humor. "Reckon this gal had something when she said she wasn't no daughter of ourn, Mom? Reckon maybe the hospital pushed somebody else's trashy kid off on us?"

In spite of Pop's voice, booming, snarling, snapping on and on, Florette finally fell asleep. It was a deep sleep, after the day's upsets, both joyous and desolating, and she woke almost too late to get ready for school.

Coral declared that she wasn't going. She couldn't bear to go. Pop bellowed at her that she should have thought of that before she done what she done. And let her try playing hooky, and so help him that belt —

Florette wondered whether the other young shoplifters would be at school, and whether their disgrace could be kept secret. It was a shock, when she and Coral approached, to see them both surrounded by a wondering group, and to hear Phyllis's voice in unashamed narration.

"And those old pussycats," she said scoffingly, "guess they never were kids. My dad always did tell me how he used to swipe watermelons and apples. Where's the big difference? And who's going to suffer from losing a pair of old gloves — ?"

Florette did not realize that she was shaking her head in vigorous denial of this philosophy until Fred's voice at her side said, "Looks like you're one of the pussycats. Don't you agree with that crazy kid, Flor?"

"Crazy is sure right," she scolded. "Don't tell me you agree with her, Fred Barlow."

"If I ever did, my mother and dad spanked it out of me in short order." He laughed, but as if he could still feel the spanking. "Anyway, I don't see how things will work very well if we don't have any rules about anything."

"And look at my sister!" Florette's body jerked in protest as Coral joined the other two girls with a jaunty toss of fair hair. "Did you know she was in it, too?" No use trying to hide it. Everyone would have to know.

"Honest, Flor? No kidding? But you mean your cousin, don't you?"

"My sister," Florette corrected, though she was sure he had known all along. "You can't go back on your own folks, no matter how they — "

"No matter how much they go back on you." Fred's blue eyes glared at Coral.

He really minds her being mean to me, Florette thought. "But I've got good news, too," she suddenly remembered to tell him. "About our Elvie."

The school bell interrupted.

"You tell me at noon," Fred called as they sped to their classrooms.

That comradeship, that sharing, made Florette forget for a while both Coral's disgrace and her flip way of dealing with it. She could look forward to noon and telling Fred all about Elvie and the Man.

After school Mr. Argon would pick up the Cochranes at the house and take them to the rehabilitation center for a get-acquainted session. Florette raced home with Fred racing with her as far as the crossroads. She arrived breathless to urge haste on Pop and Mom and to dress Elvie for the big event.

Pop had got new overalls and a new work shirt, and Mom had on her best print dress and had brushed her hair smooth.

"You both look real cool," Florette said as she scrubbed all the sections of Elvie she could reach without undressing him. Mom had put on his clean rompers, but had not noticed the floor that remained on his knees and the lunch on his face.

Florette thought with a shock of surprise that when Mom's hair was combed and she had on a girdle she didn't seem very much older than Miss Sansome. Maybe she had looked something like Coral when she was a girl. Poor Mom. Things hadn't turned out so good for her, either.

"Couldn't you leave off your cap, Pop?" she asked. "You look real good without it."

Pop scowled. He had reached a low stage today. "Don't you go trying to butter me up, young lady."

Yet when everyone was busy, Florette saw something out of the tail of her eye. Pop had paused before the mirror on Mom's dresser, and was bending his knees so he could see as he brushed his thin, fair hair. And when he strode out to Mr. Argon's car he was bareheaded.

A few minutes later the four were crowding into the shiny automobile. Mom whacked her head so sharply against the top that she subsided with pain-tightened lips, fumbling anxiously to straighten the hat that had been squashed over her eyes.

"Whyn't you just leave it off, Mom?" suggested Florette, sitting down beside her with Elvie. That hat was hardly more of an ornament than Pop's cap. "Your hair looks okay."

She guessed why Mom shook her head. A hat meant going somewhere, and Mom had been nowhere since they came to Barnett, except a few times to the old-fashioned grocery and once to the new 88¢ Store.

As Mr. Argon had told them, it was only a few minutes' ride to what Florette already hopefully called Elvie's school. Her heart thumped with expectancy and dread when she clambered out with Elvie and followed Mr. Argon, trying as she went to fluff up Elvie's curls and wipe his wet mouth. Glancing back she saw that Mom was still prodding her hat and Pop brushing back his hair.

After an introduction to a man who came out of an office at that moment, the Cochranes lost some of their stiff uncertainty. Here there was so much to see.

Florette's eyes were drawn to a long table, around

which many young children were gathered for what was evidently an afternoon snack. The children were of all sorts. Florette had never dreamed that there were so many afflicted like Elvie or in other ways. Some, like him, were jointed dolls, strung with rubber that had no elasticity. These could not hold their heads erect or control the movements of their arms and legs. Others were the exact opposite, their joints so tight that their motions were painfully stiff. Some of the limp ones steered the food unsteadily toward their mouths and missed, and laughed as if it were a gay joke. Some of the rigid ones — spastic, Mr. Argon called their condition — jerked their spoons so forcibly to their mouths that they must have bruised their lips. All were protected by apronlike bibs, and by attendants who darted here and there to lend a helping hand.

Pop's indrawn breath hissed between his teeth, and Florette thought that he was seeing that most of them were as bad off as Elvie, and many of them worse. In a husky undertone he asked, "These kids — you mean these kids can be taught?"

"Some of them can be taught as much as perfectly normal children," Mr. Argon assured him. "Others do well to be trained to take care of their own eating and drinking and their toilet habits. Had a letter today from one of our alums — " He stressed the word humorously. "He has a good position teaching school in California."

Incredulously Pop shook his head.

"It takes time," the Man warned, "time, know-how, patience."

"And spondulix," Pop added. "That's what we ain't got, mister."

"The State of Colorado doesn't aim to let any of its children suffer for lack of money. Didn't I make that clear to Florette?"

"Oh, Florrie. Yes, she said something like that, but I thought sure she'd got it wrong. Mighty little has been handed out free to us Cochranes. And we don't want no charity, mind you. But the way I've found it, the poor gets it in the neck ever' time."

"Well," said Mr. Argon, "you can pay what you are able to, and we'll make up the difference."

What we are able to! Florette thought despairingly until the Man went on.

"And if it's so you can't do anything, we'll still pay the difference. Till you get on your feet again. As I understand it, you lost your farm, Mr. Cochrane, because of all the big mechanized jobs around it?"

"That's about the size of it."

"Yes, this is a time that reminds you of the Industrial Revolution of the last century." Florette stood straighter. She knew about the Industrial Revolution now. She wondered whether Pop did. He reached up to pull the cap back on his head and, finding no cap, his hand dropped awkwardly.

Mr. Argon continued. "You have no idea how many men have been put out of work by machines. Every day they come up with a new one that can do the work of three men and do it cheaper. And it's going to be worse. It means hard times for a lot of folks until they learn new skills. But the history of civilization shows that the net result is good — Now, Miss Miller, will you let us see how you go about teaching some of these kids to walk?"

She led the way into another room, where there were long lanes with bars at each side. Here a small boy with heavy braces was being encouraged to push forward one weighted foot and then drag the other after it.

"Look, angel-baby," Florette whispered. "That's how Elvie will learn to walk."

From the protection of his sister's arms, Elvie stared at the other child. The learner grinned proudly at the visitors.

"Doing fine, Jamie!" Miss Miller praised. "Want to see another proud little man?" she asked the guests. "This will tickle you, Mr. Argon."

Vaguely Florette had been noticing strange sounds from the next room; a whirr of wheels, an occasional muffled bump, hilarious outcries. When Miss Miller ushered them in, the source of the noise was unmistakable. A boy of eight or ten was driving a wheelchair around the room, sometimes careening into a wall and shaken up like corn in a popper.

"Timmy, here are friends to see what you can do," Miss Miller greeted him, exchanging nods with the attendant nurse.

"We only just figured out a way," the nurse explained. "He has always had to have someone wheel him, and being an independent young man, he wanted to wheel himself. One of the other attendants had this bright idea—she's a spastic, that attendant."

"Well, I'll be hornswoggled," Pop muttered.

Timmy was not a spastic, but he had only stubs where legs should be, and his arms were as short. He had been set, on those stubs, down on the footrest of the wheelchair, and buckled in securely. That position brought his short arms — like nothing but flippers, Florette achingly thought — where they could manipulate the wheels. She had never seen a happier face. Cheeks red with excitement and strenuous exercise, he surveyed them with the bright-eyed triumph of a conqueror as he banged full tilt into another wall.

She felt a little like that when she speeded, the day of the fire. For a few minutes she had risen above everything that held her back.

They were taken to another room, where speech lessons were in progress. "This is desperately slow," Mr. Argon commented, "but the results are worth it."

"Like people who are in prison. Or in a cage. Being let out," said Florette. Pop looked at her wonderingly.

Miss Miller stretched coaxing hands to Elvie. "Little man, do you want to come with Miller and see what some of the other children are doing? They are learning to dress themselves," she explained to the Cochranes. "What is your boy's name? Elvie? Well, he's more like a cherub than an elf, isn't he?" She leaned closer to wipe his mouth with a clean tissue. "How they love it when they learn to keep their chins dry!"

The contact was too much for Elvie. Both wavering hands flew out as if to push away the intruder, and then went scrabbling after his sister's dress.

"Oh, Elvie," Florette besought him. "Look at the pretty lady! She will maybe be one of Elvie's teachers."

He only burrowed deeper, uttering wordless protests.

"Maybe his big sister can come with him until he gets used to us," Miss Miller suggested.

Florette's eyes went pleadingly to her father, always so set on her enduring the endless misery of school. To be sure, her eagerness for release was no longer an unmixed emotion. There was Miss Sansome, who treated her like a regular person. And there were interesting things about some of the classes. And there was Fred —

Mr. Argon was the one who brought up the matter of school. "This is an important time in the school year for Miss Florette," he said. "Less than ten days before vacation."

"Oh, yes, ten days are important in high school," Miss Miller agreed. "Maybe Elvie had better wait till vacation, since it is so near. Unless his mother —"

"Mom's poorly," Florette hastened to say, as the

197

dull red surged into Mom's face. "We'll wait, won't we, angel-baby?"

Pop talked a little on the way home. "I can't anyways get used to the idea, mister. That Elvie might learn."

"You're not alone in that, Mr. Cochrane. It's only the last few years that people have begun to understand about these brain injuries. It drives a man crazy to think of the thousands of bright-minded babies who have had to live out their lives like animals, or even like plants or vegetables. Because, you see, if you don't cultivate the growing mind, it just can't develop. I noticed you had some flowers started, Mrs. Cochrane." He turned his head slightly toward the back seat, while keeping his eyes on the highway. "If they get no water, what happens? And that's just how it is with minds. Doctors are learning to save more babies from this kind of damage, but there is still maybe one such child in each twelve hundred births. And even that means a lot of babies that need help and trained persons who work with them for years to develop their thinking power and to bypass the damaged motor cells."

Bypass. Motor cells. Would Miss Sansome be able to tell Florette what these mysteries meant?

"It would make things different for me and the Missis," Pop said slowly. "We never thought — But we always loved the little tyke." Pop straightened up and a new firmness came into his voice. "I'm thinking of set-

198

ting up in business, mister. Machine shop. I got the ear for machines, and the fingers. So has my girl Florrie" — He turned toward her — "Florrie, you think the Mister's car is humming quite like she'd ought to? Now listen to her."

Florette had already listened. "Excuse us, Mr. Argon. It's a cool car, but the mixture's too rich for the carburetor."

Mr. Argon chuckled, and winked at her in the mirror. "Miss Sansome told me what a whizz you were with motors, Florette. I'll take this buggy right into the shop and have it looked after. But as for setting up in business, Mr. Cochrane, there are a great many points to be considered."

He said no more about Pop's project, since they had reached the dump and the little house. Florette wondered about those points that needed to be considered, but she noticed that Pop's enthusiasm had not been dimmed by the Man's lack of it.

As for her, she went winging into the house, skipping so that Elvie bounced up and down and laughed himself helpless.

19

NEXT DAY a probation officer came to the little house, after telephoning to be sure that Coral and her parents would all be at home. He was a kindly-looking man, but his eyes had a way of measuring the person he was talking with, and he spoke with a firmness that made his words hard and sometimes stinging.

Since this was a first offense, the court was lenient with the three girls, but any further misbehavior would be a different matter. Another offense, and Coral would stand trial. "Do you thoroughly understand, young lady?"

"Yes, sir," Coral answered, keeping her eyes lowered.

"But she has a police record," Pop groaned. "A Cochrane with a police record."

"Not exactly," the police officer said. "She's been booked, yes, but there is not what we call a record against her. Not this first time."

"There's not going to be no second time," Pop vowed. "She knows good and well there'd be something else against her if she cut any more capers." Pop's eyes flashed from Coral to the bedroom where hung the strap.

Yet in spite of Coral's disgrace, the next to the last week of school opened more pleasantly than most.

Pop seemed happier, as if hope for his only son had lent him new life. He said that his sacred iliac was enough better so that he could do the lighter hauling without Florette's help. Pop said "sacred iliac" now with a wry smile, as if perfectly aware that the word was wrong, and using it as a joke. Florette tried to look up the word at school, but though she labored long with the fine print, she could discover no ills connected with sacredness.

Mom went around with a puckered brow, sort of puzzled but with more life to her, Florette thought.

"What you mulling over?" Pop asked Mom that Monday morning.

Mom took them by surprise. "I don't know why that woman would say Florette should be the one to come with Elvie. Hasn't he got a mom?" she inquired resentfully.

"Well, naturally, Mom, we took it for granted you wouldn't feel to go, poorly like you've been," Pop said with a funny gleam in his eyes. "It takes a young thing like Florrie—"

"You act like I was eighty," Mom snapped. "I guess I can get up enough steam to go and see that them teachers and nurses don't pick on Elvie. You want Mom to go along, don't you, Elvie?"

As for Coral, Florette could tell that she was thoroughly frightened, in spite of her mocking laughter when Pop was out of hearing. She wasn't likely to try shoplifting again. Uneasiness lifted a little from Florette's heart and left it almost free to gloat over Elvie's prospects.

"What do you look so tickled about?" Coral demanded as they walked to school that morning. "Things aren't all that cool."

"I guess not. For one thing, I'm not going to pass," Florette said. If Pop continued to insist on her staying in school — and he was likely to be even more set on it now — she faced a long, hard year.

Coral was eying her speculatively. "You won't have that Fred Barlow, either." Florette could not read her tone. "You better make hay while the sun shines. High school will be lousy with slick chicks."

As if Florette had not already thought about that. Fred was no A student, but neither was he a failing one. He would be through with ninth grade and Kennedy School this month. Florette's imagination had been filling high school classes and corridors with Jans and Phyllises, Kitties and Janes.

She edged away from discussion of her bleak year. "High school ought to be real nice for you," she said.

"With the kind of dump we live in, and no car? Nothing looks nice to me. Florrie, I've made up my mind. I'm not going to high school."

202

"But Pop—"

"This isn't the Dark Ages, when fathers could bully their daughters — beat them up, even. I've taken all I can stand. I'm going to run away."

"You wouldn't, Coral Cochrane!" Florette cried. She was imagining Coral's picture in the paper, as she had seen so many girls', and beneath it the words, like those she had heard Pop or Coral read aloud, "Missing, Coral Cochrane, age fifteen. Blond hair and blue eyes. When last seen, wearing—"

"Coral" — her voice was urgent — "you know what happens to a lot of those girls. They turn up dead as a door nail."

"I could look out for myself. I could wait tables or clerk in a store."

"Says you." Already Florette's fear had lessened. Coral was too fond of comfort and of eating to risk going on her own. "Besides," she went on, "they said in Socks that only one teen-ager out of six could get a job when they tried. Especially school dropouts. It's this darn automation. And on top of that—" she might as well pound in the facts while Coral was halfway listening — "if you run off while you're on probation, you heard what the probation officer said."

Again Coral was eying her thoughtfully. "Since when have you been taking any notice of what they say in Socks? — or in any other class except maybe Home Ec and Gym?"

"And Art. Maybe these are better teachers," Florette answered lamely. Her mind was fumbling with the question. All these years she had gradually stopped paying attention. What was the use, when she and everyone else knew how dumb she was? It had been more comfortable not to think, but to lose herself in dreams.

"Florrie" — Coral for once seemed to be thinking about her — "don't you ever wish you could be somebody? Wish it so hard it hurts? Don't you?"

Florette could not answer; not offhand. The old daydreams had been impossible ones about changing into a boy and working with machines. The newer ones had to do with a different kind of house. One like the Barlows' would be as fancy as she would want. And then — But she couldn't say any of this to Coral. She could only bite her lips and shake her head.

"Florrie, you're limping," Coral burst out, staring downward. "That place on your leg — It's awfully swollen and red. Maybe the school nurse ought to see it. I'll go with you." She spoke with resolution.

At that, Florette's eyes brimmed and she sniffed desperately. She had barely got rid of the shameful tears when they reached school.

She hadn't thought Coral would stick to her offer, but Coral did. "Look," she said to Jan and Phyl, who came to meet her, "my — Florette ran into a barbwire fence Saturday." She indicated the crisscross of adhesive bandages that partly hid the angry crimson skin. "I'm going to the nurse with her."

When the nurse uncovered the wound, Coral drew in her breath sharply. "Nasty cut," the nurse said, "and a good bit of infection. This is going to hurt, Florette."

Smiling, Florette shook her head at the sharp sting.

"Golly," said Phyl, who had been peering in at the door, "you sure got nerve, Flo. Listen, kids," she went on, "you know the annual school whingding comes Friday. Sort of corny, but fun. Let's all wear Western togs."

All day there was chatter about the picnic, which seemed to be the climax of the school year. Most of the girls and boys would ride in the school buses, but a few of the oldest boys would take their beloved little cars. The principal didn't much approve, but when the parents consented, he did not positively forbid. Students would take sack lunches, and the school would provide wieners and pop and something for dessert.

Florette and Coral found excitement at home, also. Mr. Argon had telephoned, suggesting that Pop and Mom take Elvie to the Center that morning if they could arrange to. And that was what they had done.

Florette picked Elvie up, gazing at him as if she had lost something precious. "Without Sister!"

He settled into her arms with a great sigh.

"Plumb wore to a frazzle," Pop said. "But your mom says he done real good. Mom is pooped, herself."

"It's just till he gets kind of uset to the folks there," Mom said. Though her flushed face was tired, there was in it again that look of being awake. "It's funny how they do. But kind of interesting."

"Your mom told 'em it would be nice if you could come for a few days after school was out, Florrie," Pop said, "so's you could catch on to some of the new tricks. Like not calling him a baby no more. They're sure set on that. No, sir! Elvie's a big boy now."

The talk about Elvie put everything else out of mind till supper was over. They'd even talked while they ate, and that was unusual for the Cochranes.

"Oh — the school picnic!" Coral exclaimed, and ran into her room and Florette's, to fling things out of her dresser drawer. "The kids are going Western. Florrie, you got any good jeans I can wear?"

"No, nor any decent ones for my own self."

"Pop, that means I got to get new levis and a checked shirt."

"If they don't decide to put you in jail," Pop said harshly. "Wouldn't need no picnic clo'es then."

"Oh, Pop, quit talking like that." Coral put her hands over her ears. "The boys say the worst they'll do is keep us on probation."

"Well, far as clo'es go, looks like Florrie's got the first call on money for new clo'es. She's sure wore her overalls ragged, helping me haul and h'ist."

Coral came out, pouting prettily, and smoothed back Pop's hair from his lined forehead. "Oh, Pop, you know very well I meant we both would have to have new jeans and shirts."

Though Pop grunted and jerked his head away, he seldom could resist Coral's coaxing. "Well, the both of you can go to town tomorrow and pick yourselves out what you got to have. But mind you don't get the kind that go to pieces first time they're washed. Nor the skin-tight pants I seen on some girls."

Florette pulled her levis and shirt from the hook behind their bedroom door, and scrutinized them. "I did sort of set my heart on a dress for church — Jane asked us again — but I don't reckon these would quite do — "

The pants were faded to a pale blue, and had holes in both knees. "I could get those patches at the Dime Store," she said. "Some of the kids wear them for trimming. On brand-new overalls and shirts, even."

"But you've grown so they're halfway to your knees. Pop," Coral shrieked, "I'd be shamed to death if my own sister went to the school party looking like a scarecrow."

"Oh, so she's turned into your sister again?" Pop's soft look at Coral had hardened. "Reckon it's since you was hauled off to the police station you've decided you wasn't too la-de-da for the rest of us. That it? I say, is that it?"

"You know I was kidding."

"In a pig's eye you were." Vigorously Pop knocked the ashes from his pipe. "But I reckon you got to get the duds, Florrie. Them work clo'es ain't hardly decent."

207

Next morning he poured the money into Florette's hand. "Want I should pick you up at school and run you over to Penney's?"

Coral drew down an expressive mouth. "In that old rattletrap? I think Jane will take us."

Jane did. She also was to buy a new outfit.

"But you've got swell slacks," Coral reminded her. "And that dreamy silk shirt."

"Too sissy. Rather have jeans and plaid cotton."

Shopping was fun. Florette had almost forgotten what it was like to have new denim levis, deep blue with bright red stitching, and their own clean new smell. As for the shirt, she had been wearing one of Pop's that had shrunk. Pop was of slender build, so it hadn't had to shrink much to fit Florette. But it had faded to no-color, and now she joyously picked out a Hawaiian print in splashy orange and blue.

"But those colors are almost sure to run." Jane warned. "You get one of this other brand and it won't fade."

Funny, Florette thought: Jane could buy new clothes whenever she liked, but she was more particular about their lasting than were the Cochranes. Reluctantly Florette laid aside the clamorous green palm trees and blue sky and orange sand.

"Look," said Jane, examining a label. "Here's one that would look swell on you. Like your gym suit."

"Pop will make out I've caught on fire," Florette

demurred. But she grew warm with pleasure when she laid the bittersweet-colored garment with the jeans.

When she wore the outfit to school on the day of the picnic, Fred gave a wolf whistle and collapsed on the ground.

"You get straight up out of that dirt, Fred Barlow," she scolded enjoyably. "In your new clothes, too. Couldn't you pick a cleaner place to fall?"

It had been her very first wolf whistle.

School was dismissed after lunch that day, to give more time for the picnic. A flock of the familiar school buses were waiting when the students poured out, laughing and chattering and gay in their Western garb. Besides the buses, there were a few small cars, as expected, some of them looking as if they had come straight from the dump.

Coral climbed into one of these, while her sister stared open-mouthed. "She's so easy shamed," she said to Fred. "And that car looks worse than Pop's truck."

It was painted in ragged stripes of red white and blue, and decorated with hearts, and with inscriptions lettered in staggering capitals: ROCK AND ROLL, GIVE US LIBARTY, and KEEP OFF: DINAMYTE.

"It's the style," Fred informed Florette. "Anything's okay if it's the style."

"I don't like the sound of it," Florette objected. "Listen at that engine. Corrie! Corrie! You better not — "

Coral was laughing too loud to hear anything outside

the hot rod. And Fred was pulling at Florette's new sleeve and urging, "Let her be, Flor. Are you your sister's keeper?"

"She sure needs one." But Florette climbed into the bus as Fred pushed her.

It was exciting. They sang and shouted till the driver stopped the bus and turned to tell them that he couldn't hear himself think, and couldn't tell whether the old engine was hitting on two or ten. Now and then Florette caught sight of the red, white and blue jalopy. It was jammed full, and an extra boy hung on each of the ramshackle running boards. When it climbed a hill it dropped behind the buses. When it reached the top, it shot giddily past them down the steep incline.

"He's got no brakes," fumed Florette. "Why don't he put her in second?"

"Well, you can't do a thing about it, Miss Know-It-All," Fred assured her. "And don't you remember what the Bible says — or is it Bill Shake-the-Spear — anyway that about the Lord taking care of children and fools?"

"Reckon He's got a double job with Coral, then. And if it was Him sent Miss Sansome to keep her from getting into that rambling wreck — well, I saw her trying, but Coral got away." Florette spole gayly, and soon she found herself feeling gay. "It's getting real pretty," she exclaimed as they came into a stretch of canyon where a brook danced downhill beside the road and aspen trees fluttered bright green leaves at the passersby.

"Cool," Fred agreed. "But it's even nicer when we get higher, don't you think?"

"I've never been this high before," Florette admitted.

20

"Gosh!" Fred was incredulous. "You never been up one of the canyons yet, Flor? Real often on Sundays Dad takes us up to places like Wild Basin, and we have a cookout. Swell up there. And you're so gone on flowers, you'd be daffy over the lady's slippers I found once, and the gentians. We often take along a couple kids — "

"That Perry girl, I reckon."

Fred laughed. "Not yet I haven't. Usually it's one of the fellows. But Mother says you're okay, Flor. And Pop's all fixed to like you. He says I've changed for the better since I've been walking you home. Not much better, but some."

Everything was wonderful. Florette was in a daze of happiness. For a while she sat watching and laughing at the antics which, as the driver had said, hardly let you hear yourself think. And she was a part of it, a part of this noisy gaiety. Occasionally something would pull her eyes away from the crowd to the window and the passing scene. "The brook makes such a fuss," she commented. "As if it was having a heap of fun and wanted everybody to look at it."

Sometimes the scene opened out on a mountain meadow, with sleek black cattle grazing on the new grass, and a plank bridge leading over the now quiet brook to a house nestled against the hills and surrounded by evergreens and aspens. "It would be neat to live in a place like that," said Florette, "with Angus cattle and — see the black-nose sheep and the little lambs." She swiveled to get the last look at them. "And those Duroc hogs. Their little pigs are as cute as babies. Wouldn't Elvie love them!"

"Gosh, you know all their names and addresses," Fred teased her. "You could call them anchovies and peppermints for all I'd know."

Florette made a face at him, thinking she would try to remember to tell Pop that joke. If Pop was in a good mood. "I'm a farmer's daughter, that's why," she said.

They passed abandoned farms, with buildings leaning exhaustedly or lying collapsed, and old fences, silver-gray with weather, laid like featherstitching. "I bet Pop could fix up that house so a person could live in it," Florette said, as they passed a dilapidated specimen. "If his back got better. And if he starts up his own business like he's talking. That fence!" she broke off. "Mom showed us how to make fences like that. With old-fashioned clothespins. On the kitchen floor." Hard to imagine Mom down on the floor making fences.

Her thoughts were halted by a banging jolt. She bounced upward and came down hard as the bus clattered over a bridge that crossed a small gully. With another crash the wheels struck what must have been a washed-out dip at the upper end and sent half the smaller children off on the floor.

"You'd think they'd put in a new bridge there," Florette said, straightening herself in her seat. "That one must be almost as rough as the one leading over to the old barn yonder, the one that looks at least a hundred years old."

They continued to climb, angling around hairpin curves and sometimes drawing up against a rocky cliff until a descending vehicle could edge past them. After a particularly steep half mile, followed by a gentler ascent, they came out on another meadow, with a small, quiet stream winding through it.

Here the caravan stopped and spilled out its occupants, who dashed to and fro, stretching cramped legs and releasing effervescent spirits in shrieks and shouts. Florette and Fred raced here and there with the rest, picking up firewood as they ran.

"Always think there's going to be wood to burn — hey! I made a pun: wood to burn, get it? — and usually it's as scarce as hen's teeth. Say, Flor, why is it you always elect yourself to a job? Look at your sister. Ever see her around where there's work to do?"

Florette had no trouble looking at Coral. She was still in Sid's car, which was hiccuping away from the assembly and up into a rough, narrow road.

"Sid! Clint! Sam!" Miss Sansome called. One of

the bus drivers set fingers to teeth and loosed a piercing whistle. It was like a whisper when a jet plane was taking off.

"They'll come running when they see the smoke," the driver said. "Nothing hollers as loud as an empty stomach. Besides, I know that old mine road. It's overgrown so bad they can't get far."

Preparations went on. Barnett's park service provided stone barbecue stoves in all such picnic areas, since forest fires were always a threat. Some of the Scouts built fires in several stoves, and by the time they were at the roasting stage, and boys and drivers had collected and sharpened enough wiener sticks, the pop bottles were waiting on the tables and lunches from the sacks piled on paper plates.

Still Sid's jalopy had not reappeared, and Florette and Fred went loping over to the old road. From its foot they could hear shrieks of laughter, warning shouts, cracking and snapping of twigs and branches.

"Mercy to us!" Florette appealed to everything and nothing. "They must be trying to back down. Listen at the racket."

When the gay vehicle appeared, they could see that it was indeed backing. The boys who had clung to the running boards were scrambling and tumbling down the road, waving their arms and yelling incoherent advice: "To the left, Sid, — no, I mean right. Ouch, that hurt! Now straighten her out."

Those in the car were pressing toward the center,

ducking their heads, clutching each other and squealing.

"Gosh, he'll never make it!" Fred cried with the thick end of his changing voice. "Flor, you keep clear of the crazy nuts."

With a final rush, and a squall of ineffectual brakes, the little car racketed into the open, aiming toward the campfires and tables, from which came other squeals and shouts. It was only when it reached the level that it stopped.

"Who said I couldn't do it?" bragged Sid's falsetto. "Miss Sansome, whadda you bet your brand-new Corvette wouldn't have made it so slick?"

"Heaven forbid!" Miss Sansome was fervent. "It would mean a paint job on both sides."

"It's only the girls who need a paint job here," hooted Sam, jerking a thumb toward Coral, who was deftly applying lipstick.

Lucky her shirt was new, strong gingham, Florette thought, or it would have been torn to ribbons.

"It was awful," Corinne cried in delicious horror. "It got narrower and narrower, and the bushes closer and closer, and not any place to turn around."

"I never thought the brakes would hold on that grade," marveled Florette. "Reckon they wouldn't, if the trees hadn't grabbed you."

"Brakes? Got no brakes," boasted Sid. "More kicks without."

216

"Coral, you won't ride downhill in that heap?" Florette called worriedly. "Pop would be fit to be tied."

"What Pop doesn't know won't hurt him," Coral answered, going with Sid and the others to get wieners and sticks.

Soon they were all maneuvering for good places, according to their disposition and experience. Some chose the hottest flames, and their voices soon rose in protest as their meat caught fire. They waved the flaming torches so vigorously that the flying juices called forth indignant squalls from their neighbors. Others shrank so timidly from the heat that their wieners remained smooth, slim cylinders, like varnished cattails. Still others chose corners where only glowing embers remained.

"You're burning yours to a coal, Fred Barlow," Florette scolded, leaving her own propped up and roasting gently while she worked a fresh one on a stick for a twelve-year-old with scorched fingers.

"Like it that way, smarty." Fred stuck it into a roll and jammed half the sandwich into his mouth. "Charcoal's — good for you," he added with difficulty.

Florette's had split open and dripped with a delicious sizzle on the charcoal. "Don't you wish you had mine?" she asked, encasing it in a roll and anointing it with mustard. Why was it she had never before been able to kid anybody?

"Here's your Coke," said Fred, presenting an opened

217

bottle with a flourish, but refusing to admire her cookery.

Dessert was made with marshmallows exposed to the same fires and pressed between graham crackers.

"You think you're so smart," Fred teased Florette. "Most of the rest of us have charcoal again, and your marshmallow is as brown and puffy as a — as a toasted cloud."

Florette could hardly bear to have the afternoon end. They sang school songs, and "green tree growing all round," and others that everyone knew. While Florette sang, she was helping carry water from the stream to douse the fires.

By that time the segment of western sky visible between mountains and trees told them by its color that they must be on their way.

"Let's nab a good seat," said Fred. "Best ones are about second from the front."

"I got to make Corrie get on a bus. Honest, Fred, it's no joke about that old rattletrap of Sid's. The brakes are clean gone, just like he said."

"If it's all that bad, I better go and put one of the men wise," Fred said doubtfully, "and have the fellows call me tattletale."

Florette was already hunting her sister. She caught sight of her, in the flag-colored car again, between Sid and Sam, and with three boys and a girl jammed into the back seat.

Florette pushed through the crowd toward the car. "Corrie! Corrie!" she shouted. Even her strong young voice did not pierce the clamor, and everyone in the jalopy was intent on what Sid was doing. He was turning the car and steering it toward the homeward road.

The boys in the back seat were leaning forward, giving advice between shouts of laughter, while Sid fiddled with the mechanism before him and turned his head to yell replies. None of them took any notice of the men teachers and drivers who were running toward them with yells and waving arms.

Florette was far ahead of the men. She had scrambled through to the open space around the car when it began to roll down that first gentle slope. Her mouth opened in a scream of protest as the jalopy poised and teetered on the brink of the sharp downward incline.

Sid was pushing with feet and hands, and his face had gone white.

" 'Mergency! 'Mergency!" shrieked Florette.

Sid was scrambling out of the car.

"No. Stay by her, Sid!" Florette called.

He stumbled away, while Sam fell out of the other side.

"Jump, Corrie, jump!" Florette screamed, leaping forward. Coral sat like one frozen, while the boys and girls in the back seat struggled with the doors, which were wired shut.

The men were nearly there, but Florette was ahead

219

of them. She leaped toward the doorless front, grabbed at a hinge that tore her hand, held on, making giant, leaping strides, pulled herself in. The shouts, roars, shrieks of the pursuers died behind them as the jalopy picked up speed on that dizzy descent.

Mechanically Florette had set her foot hard on the useless brake. She groped for the emergency, gasped with relief when she found it and pulled it back as far as it would go. No slackening — faster and faster.

"Corrie, honk the horn."

She might as well have commanded a doll.

"You back there — reach over — keep the horn going —"

After a fumbling moment a boy hung over the front seat and seized the old-fashioned bulb. The careening vehicle emitted a continuous deafening blast. Ahead of them a car skittered up against a high bank and stopped, its driver shaking his fist. Another clung perilously to the edge of the abyss.

"Corrie — grab something — put head on knees. You kids, hold on — I can't do nothing — but steer —"

With no windshield, Florette's heavy hair streamed behind her. Her eyelashes were blown backward, and sand peppered her face and filled her eyes, blinking desperately to clear themselves.

Her thoughts raced ahead of the car. The dip they struck on the way up, just after they crossed the banging old bridge — would they go crashing into the end of the bridge there? Overturn?

Around those hairpin curves she steered the flying car, thankful that most of them were well banked, gritting her teeth and swaying to the outer edge of those that were not.

"I'm going to jump!" shrieked the girl in the back seat.

"Don't you dare!" Florette cried. "This fast — kill you — "

"Good as dead already," croaked a boy.

Florette shook her head. "No! Got a chance!"

"God, if you care — show me what to do —" she was saying, aloud.

Then, off at her right, the gray fence marking the edge of the abandoned farm and the level sweep of barnyard, the shackly bridge leading toward it —

Better than crashing into a rock. Or even into the end of the regular bridge —

"Hold on, kids — "

Swerving off the road to the right she struck the farm bridge with a deafening clatter of boards. She gave the car gas with foot pounding the floor — it was slipping back — it was across —

With a world-filling crash it burst through the fence and into the sagging barn.

And that was all Florette knew.

21

Florette pulled open her eyes. Her pillow must have got over her head and covered one of them, but she couldn't seem to get up strength enough to push it away. Her arms were heavy as lead. Anyway, she wasn't awake. Her uncovered eye was looking straight up at a surface as smooth and unscarred as new snow — pale green snow. There was nothing like that in her bedroom, so she must be dreaming.

A voice close beside her said, "She opened her eyes — "

Nice to have Miss Sansome's voice in her dream. Only — worried-sounding.

They wouldn't let her settle back into the dream deep enough to drown the pain. She never had headaches. And this wasn't exactly a headache: it was an everything-ache. She twitched her heavy arms and her shoulders shrieked at her —

A hand came and rested gently on a piece of her forehead. Cool. Smooth and cool. Good-smelling.

"Can you hear me, Florette?" asked Miss Sansome's voice.

Florette opened the free eye and looked up into the

kindness of Miss Sansome's face. "She's really conscious, nurse."

Florette tried to remember, but all she could fish out of the maze of her mind was the racket of boards and the crash and splintering of wood, going on and on. She couldn't find words to ask, but as if her eye were putting the question, Miss Sansome answered a part of it.

"The doctor said it was a concussion, a bad one. But you are coming out of it all right."

With tremendous effort Florette's lips, which felt stiff and swollen, shaped a name: "Corrie?"

Miss Sansome replied quickly. "Your sister was taken home yesterday. Not a thing but scratches and one deep cut where a splintered board ripped her arm. The others are okay, too." Miss Sansome's voice shook, and tears brimmed her eyes. "You — you little peach," she said.

"It was — yesterday?" Florette whispered.

"This is the third day, Florette. Your pop was here all the first night, and then he stayed home with Elvie and let your mother come. You see they weren't sure yet — Someone else has been haunting the place, too," she teased. "Those are his flowers. He wanted you to see them when you woke up."

Florette's eyes moved stiffly in the direction Miss Sansome indicated. On the long narrow table now swiveled across the foot of the bed, among ordinary useful

223

things like a carafe of water and a box of Kleenex, stood a vase, with three roses. Kind of orange color.

She'd never had any roses before. Florist's roses. From a boy, too.

"Go to sleep, honey," Miss Sansome said. "I'll tell that Fred Barlow he'll have to wait till next time you're awake."

When Florrie wakened, she felt a wetness on her face, and heard little whimpering cries. Her heart joggled happily, and she opened her eye. "Elvie! Elvie-angel!"

Pop was holding Elvie suspended above the bed, and he had touched her cheek with his little wet mouth.

"Trust him to know his big sis," Pop blubbered. "Even with nothing showing but one eye. Fit to be tied, Elvie's been."

"It — wouldn't hurt to — put him down — on the bed?" Florette whispered.

"I guess it will be okay," the nurse said doubtfully.

"Be real still, Elvie," Pop cautioned, gently laying him down. His head went burrowing into Florette's neck in spite of the bandages, and his hands fluttered to caress her.

"Here's Mom," Pop said, standing aside.

Mom looked different again. It wasn't only that she had put on a girdle and combed her hair. "Florrie," she gulped, "Florrie."

And over Mom's shoulder Coral was peering, a Coral with a plaster on her cheek and another on her forehead and a bandage from wrist to shoulder. "Florrie," she said almost resentfully, "I guess you saved my life. I guess you saved all our lives." She didn't say it graciously. She said it almost accusingly. But she pushed past her mother and kissed Florette, a funny kiss, more like an angry peck. But it was the first kiss Florette could remember from her since they were little. Before Florette could say or do anything, Coral had turned and run from the room.

Not until the next day did they let Fred come in, and he surprised her, too. He stood staring down at her. "Gosh, but do you ever look good!" he blurted. "We none of us thought — when we lifted you out — You sure look good to me."

"I must," Florette said. "They were scared I'd — break the looking glass. Never — gave me — a peek."

"Sit down, young man," said the nurse, indicating a chair. "You can talk to her. Just a little while."

"Thanks — for the roses."

"Think nothing of it," said Fred, sitting with a hand spread on each knee. He looked at her, and at the roses, and at a tree outside the window. "Nice room," he said.

"Real nice," Florette agreed, and looked around as far as she could wondering about it for the first time. "Mercy to us!" she stammered. "How can Pop — ? Not even — a ward. Must cost — five dollars a day!" Shock loosened her stiff tongue.

"Eighteen. But gosh," Fred said with feeling, "you think when someone saves three boys and a girl's life, to say nothing of her own sister, — do you suppose their folks are likely to let them put a person like that in a ward?"

"Mercy to us."

After a little while she tried again. "Fred — do you know — just what — happened? Nobody — told me."

"You came to the right man to ask that question, girl. It's like this: I jump into one of the other hot rods, me and a bus driver and a couple teachers, and we follow you down. Golly, but you'd busted that old fence and barn like nobody's business. That barn had really given up: fell down over you and the car and the other kids. When we got there the kids were pulling themselves out of that mess of broken boards. Corinne and Coral were having hysterics. I didn't pay much mind to the dumb clucks. Gosh, Flor!"

Florette's interest was growing. "Where — was I at?"

"Jammed in under the steering wheel, practically covered with blood — that cut on your forehead. And limp as a rag. Out like a light, and we all thought — "

Florette shut her eye, because it seemed to be getting silly and wet.

The nurse spoke quickly. "That cut won't spoil your pretty face. The only scar will be above the eyebrow."

"No pretty face — to spoil." Amusement dried the tears. "Now if — it had been — Coral's — "

"Says you," Fred said gruffly. "Yours is nicer than

any old pretty face." He was out of his chair and rushing to the door as he spoke, almost as Coral had rushed.

Both the nurse and Florette giggled: Fred had looked so shocked at what he had said. It was nice, Florette thought. The aching and the stiffness were not too much to pay. Unless —

"Is anything — broken bad?" she asked. "Can I — can I walk? My legs do feel — "

"It's only the bandages," the nurse hurried to reassure her. "You've been X-rayed and everything is okay. It was just that the boards ripped your legs pretty deeply. And there was the concussion, of course. The concussion was the danger, but that danger is past."

Next day other wonderful things happened. A brisk young woman with a camera appeared at Florette's bedside and took pictures from every angle, with flaring flashlights that sent Florette's eye snapping shut.

"Be funny-looking, all — bandaged thisaway." Florette appealed to the nurse. "Whatever does she want them for?" She was talking now with little effort.

"You'll see. In the newspaper. Tomorrow night, likely."

"My pitcher — in the paper?" It was almost too much. She hoped the bed jacket would show. She touched it lovingly, soft as a kitten's fur, and blue like a flower. Miss Sansome had tried to find bittersweet color, but had taken the blue as second choice, remembering how much Florette liked blue flowers.

"We have to keep you prettied up," the nurse said, "You have so many visitors, being a heroine and all. A gang of kids under twelve were so mad at us because it was against the rules for us to let them in. They left this bunch of wildflowers. Had to get a bucket to put them in, there were so many. Look: lupine and golden banner, and a lot of other kinds."

By that time the cards came in floods. Several were from Jane's church school class, most of them saying that they all looked forward to her being with them again, her and her sister.

A few presents appeared, besides: perfume, writing paper, handkerchiefs. Most exciting was the box Miss Sansome brought, a big one wrapped in fancy paper and with ribbon rosettes like flowers. The card said, "From the grateful parents of the crazy kids in Sid's deceased car."

"Deceased?" Florette puzzled.

"Dead and not lamented," Miss Sansome said.

"They needn't of." Florette was working at the ribbons with stiff fingers, lately released from the bandages.

"Oh, needn't they!" Miss Sansome spoke with good-natured scorn. "Shall I lend a hand with those tricky tapes? Or do you want to do it yourself?"

Florette ducked a shy little nod and went on fumbling. When the box was open a cloud of white tissue paper must still be folded back. And then —

"Mercy to us!" Florette choked.

228

Miss Sansome held it up for her, a sweater set, soft as the bed jacket, and a skirt to match. "Bittersweet color," Miss Sansome said, peering at it with satisfaction.

Florette was blissfully crying.

Pop came in just then, carrying the same old cap but wearing a clean shirt. He scowled at the fragrant cloud of color Miss Sansome was spreading on the bed.

"Where'd that come from?" he growled. "Mrs., I always took care of my family myself. No relief, even. One thing you can say for us Cochranes: we don't mooch. Sometimes we ain't got much but beans in the kitchen, but we don't have to go whining to Welfare. Florrie don't need other folks' clo'es. Coral helped me pick out a dress for her. Want me to fetch it next time I come, Florrie?" He glared anew at the sweaters and skirt when Florette instinctively clutched them to her.

"But these are just a loving gift, Mr. Cochrane," Miss Sansome interposed. "Like flowers or candy. Seems as if," she said, with the twinkle which often marked her everyday talk, "seems as if the fool kids who made her tear her new Westerns into a fringe — well, the least they can do is to replace what they spoiled."

Pop relaxed slightly. "But just you wait, Mrs. Sansome. Just you wait till I set up my own business, like I plan to. Me and Florrie will make things hum, oncet I set up that little machine shop."

At that point happened the first unpleasant thing in

the five days — not counting the aches and pains, since they had brought so much that was new and wonderful. It was Mr. Argon who injected the drop of bitterness.

"Excuse me," he said, coming into the room. "I couldn't help overhearing, Mr. Cochrane, and I beg leave to disagree with you. This isn't the time to start a new business. Not for you," he added bluntly.

Pop's blue eyes were bright with wrath. "So you think I ain't up to it? Well, if you don't mind my saying so right out — like you just did — I couldn't hardly care less."

"Now, now," said the Man, "it's nothing against you, Cochrane. Some folks are made to run a business and some aren't. I hate to think where I'd land if I set up for myself."

Pop was sputtering, and the nurse and Miss Sansome were making uneasy motions toward Florette, but Mr. Argon plowed ahead.

"When you come to look over the ground, you'll see what I see: a machine shop on every second corner."

"With dumb mechanics. Now me and Florrie — "

"You and Florette are special," Mr. Argon soothed him. "I know that very well. That's why I bet you — bet you a nickel and a dime — that you can get yourself a good paying job in one of the shops already there. I mean a really good paying job." He named a sum that made Florette stare incredulously. "Because it's one kind of service that's in short supply in Barnett: too many garages but not enough skilled mechanics. I looked into it."

Pop muttered something under his breath about thanking Mr. Argon kindly, but not caring to take any more of his time looking after what was Pop's own business. Still, the sum Mr. Argon mentioned had had a calming effect, and when he started out a few minutes later, he was twirling his cap in the way Florette recognized as a sign of deep thought.

That was not all. Slowly he turned as he reached the door. "Mister," he asked, his eyes fixed on his own hands, "that any special shop I should ask at? For me, I darn well wouldn't change my plans and knuckle under to nobody. But Florette here, well, she's kind of set her heart on paint and lonillium and such — "

Mr. Argon said, "Sure thing, Mr. Cochrane. Ask at Bill's place, on Sixteenth and Rock. Tell him you're the mechanic I told him about."

When Pop had finally gone, Mr. Argon said to the nurse, "After I stirred up such a ruckus maybe you won't feel like letting me stay any longer. But I've got good news for our young lady."

"Our young lady is doing so well I guess a little more visiting won't hurt her."

"Mind if I stay, too?" Miss Sansome was folding the sweaters with care, but still looking at Mr. Argon as if she were almost as much vexed with him as pleased.

"Definitely not. You're a part of it. I hope I didn't

231

make you feel bad, Florette. But you'd be surprised at the number of small businesses that sprouted and withered only last year. And you know your father — "

"Pop has — what is it they say? A green finger? Like Grampa and Great-Grampa. But I reckon — " Florette spoke reluctantly — "he isn't so much for business. He never did have a way with him when it come to selling crops and like that. And he gets all worked up over such things as that paper-baler — " Mr. Argon looked inquiring, but did not stop her for an explanation — "All the same, I always did think it would be nice — if I could be partners with Pop — and work with machinery — "

Mr. Argon's blue-green marble eyes almost hid themselves in his smile. "What would you say to taking vocational training next fall, young lady? Polishing up on the fine points of mechanics?"

Reproachfully Miss Sansome broke in. "But, Mr. Argon! You know we haven't been able to get that vocational school started here. What we have doesn't amount to a row of pins."

"Not as of yesterday," Mr. Argon crowed. "Not as of yesterday, much as we've been hammering away at it. But Florette here has precipitated a crisis." He laughed aloud at Florette's puzzled frown. "Coon Valley School District needed something to joggle it out of its lethargy — its plain laziness. And you're it. Vocational training, on a worthwhile scale, will open up next fall with a good course in mechanics. Nothing yet specifically for girls — ordinary girls. But you, my dear child, will be the first student enrolled, if the idea pleases you."

Florette's incredulous glow was suddenly quenched. "Is it because I'm so dumb at everything else?" she mumbled. "Because I can't read even as good as ten-year-old kids?"

"Oh, come come come!" Mr. Argon sounded as if tears terrified him. "You've got to get that idea out of your head pronto. That's what Miss Sansome here put us next to. She said nobody could be so smart other ways and not be able to read — "

"But — but it's true," Florette mumbled.

"Maybe you didn't know it," the Man continued, "though maybe you guessed I was up to something. But I gave you a pretty fair I.Q. test when we were trying to get your little brother used to me. I wanted to see for myself. As I told you, Miss Sansome, I used one of the newer tests, the kind that depends less than formerly on verbal skills. And as you said, this girl is all there. Might as well call me a dunce because I never could thread a needle," he sputtered.

Florette opened her free eye. "But the reading — ?"

"Didn't anyone ever tell you that you're what they call a mirror reader?"

"Mirror — ? Whatever is that?"

Mr. Argon shook his head. "It's rather mysterious even now, though many smart people have been afflicted with something of the sort. The most noticeable form is when a person tends to read from right to left, as in a mirror. But there are all kinds of variations. Most often it occurs in people who are either left-handed or both-handed — what we call ambidextrous. You, I take it, don't see the letters set in a line —"

"Jiggly." Florette's eyes were wide and eager. "Jumping around. Don't they act that way for you? Machines you can take hold of, but not letters. Mister, can they cure it?"

"Not exactly cure it," he admitted. "But they can help you get used to it. You can go to remedial reading classes. You can get so you read much more comfortably."

"But not everybody has to be a great reader," Miss Sansome put in. "Some are book-minded and some are — well, hand-minded. You know how many times I've said I wished I could have a little of your hand-cleverness. But I guess it's really true that it takes all kinds."

"To make a world," Mr. Argon finished the saying. "That's it, girl. It's up to you to make a world out of this mess of scrap metal we've turned things into. It's up to you."

"Who? Me?" This was big. It was too big. Florette looked past him at the door. There stood Fred, awkwardly braced on one foot, as if again about to run. The large box in his hands must be candy.

"This is the happiest day of my whole life," said Florette.